CHOKECHERRY VALLEY LOVE

JEAN REZAB

For Mike, Pat, Theresa, Ron, and Jack

My favorite siblings

Books by Jean Rezab

Richmond Sibling Series

Chokecherry Valley Comfort
Chokecherry Valley Joy
Chokecherry Valley Love
Chokecherry Valley Faith

Other Books

In This Place Together
The Prediction

ACKNOWLEDGMENTS

Special thanks to the excellent editor, Krista Venero at Mountains Wanted Publishing & Indie Author Services for great suggestions. She helped create a better book than I could have envisioned on my own.

Thank you to the book cover artist at Sunset Rose Books for an amazing cover.

Considerable thanks to my family who have encouraged me in my writing journey.

Thank you to Sally, Ruth, and Amy, great friends who are also great at running book ideas and cover designs past. I couldn't have finished this book without your help.

Special thanks to Connie Victoria Volk for helping by editing and making suggestions for a stronger book. She writes her own books. www.connievolk.com

CHAPTER 1

Wednesday Ashley hurried into the almost full classroom and her heart started beating even faster in her ears. She should have taken Oral Communications when she was a freshman, but she'd put it off because she hated to speak in front of others.

In addition to her fear of speaking, she preferred getting to class early to choose a desk in the back of the room. Today, she'd been delayed after her previous class by a classmate who wanted to talk, and she had a hard time getting away from her heartbreaking story. Ashley's choices came down to a desk in the center of one row in the middle of the room or the desk in the front row next to a guy whose feet splayed way out in front of him. He was tall, or else the slumped posture made him seem that way. He appeared to be sleeping.

Oh, well. She sat next to him as the noise level around her continued at a steady rhythm of books slapping on desks, along with laughter and voices. At least the sleeper wouldn't be snickering with friends or looking at his phone during the upcoming lecture. She pulled out her notebook and hung her backpack on her chair.

A minute later, the instructor walked into the room and stood behind the podium. She'd never had Dr. Williams as a teacher, but she'd heard he ran a strict but fair class. The sudden decrease in noise level showed most of the students had listened to the stories from prior students.

Dr. Williams looked at the sleeping guy next to her. She didn't know what possessed her, but she reached out and jabbed him in the arm with her finger.

He startled awake and looked around. Then, with a sheepish grin, he sat up straight and eyed the teacher. "Sorry." His voice came out gravelly and deep.

Ashley found herself intrigued by his immediate way of taking responsibility and she might turn out to like the guy. His dark hair emphasized his brown eyes, and they looked clear, if dazed. They weren't red, which meant he probably wasn't sleeping off a late night due to drinking.

She noticed his age because he was an older student like herself. At twenty-seven, she was one of the oldest students in most of the classes she took. In addition, freshmen usually took Oral Communications to get it over with, which especially highlighted the difference in age between her and the other students in this class. Her advisor for her psychology undergraduate degree had pointed out the class each semester they met to go over her schedule.

Dr. Williams looked at her and asked, "Do you know him?"

"No," she murmured.

"Well, if he drifts off again, you have my permission to poke him." He nodded at her and then the guy. He pulled a stack of papers out of his briefcase. He handed the stack to the girl at the end of the front row. "Please pass these around."

As the papers were being handed down the row, Dr. Williams said, "You'll need the first book for the four speeches you'll give in the class. Below that, you'll find the suggested reading for additional help with any of the speeches. I don't care how you get the book. Beg, borrow, but don't steal."

Ashley began to like Dr. William's sly humor.

"Seriously," he continued, "if you can't find a copy of any of this information, please let me know. I want everyone to have a fair chance at passing this class. Please write your name and your email on a sheet of paper and leave it on my desk on your way out. I usually don't bring paper to class. I send everything by email."

After that, she missed most of the following lecture on the different speeches, and it turned out to be the longest thirty minutes Ashley spent in a long time. The harder she tried to pay attention to the instructor, the more she wanted to talk to the guy next to her and find out his story.

When Dr. Williams dismissed class, she grabbed her notebook and backpack and quickly slid from her desk to hurry out of the room. She didn't realize the guy who sat next to her was following her until he said, "Hey, wait."

She glanced behind her and met his gaze. For a second, she stopped, stunned by the brown of his eyes, and then forced herself to continue out the door. "Sorry, we can't hold up traffic here."

When she got into the hallway, she moved along the corridor away from the door. "I don't have much time," she said. "I have an appointment."

"I wanted to thank you. Dr. Williams found my nap amusing, but I don't imagine he would have if you hadn't done the finger jab to my shoulder." He smiled at her.

She found his grin as fascinating as his brown eyes. She couldn't believe how attracted she was to him, and she didn't even know his name—which she should find out, and then get going. "He did seem amused. I do have to get to an appointment. Maybe we can talk more before class on Friday. Would that work for you?"

"Sounds great. I'm Jason."

"Hi, Jason. I'm Ashley. See you Friday. I have to run." She forced herself to turn away from him and hurried down the hallway to the outside door. She was going to be late if she didn't run when she got outside.

#

The cool fall afternoon felt good after the heated classroom. Early September could be any temperature between freezing and a hundred degrees. Today was in the low sixties. No need for a jacket if she didn't linger too long, and if she stood in the sun, the temperature was perfect. She loved the sixties and low seventies, and September and October were her favorite months.

Ashley met with her class advisor, who kept her fully engaged. They discussed her forty-hour clinical observation at St. Gertrude's Medical

Center, where she'd observe in the Social Work Department and then the Mental Health Unit every afternoon starting at 1:00 p.m. Because she could only get in four hours a day, the time at St. Gertrude's Medical Center would actually take two weeks instead of one week. Her oldest brother, Paul, worked as a physician there, and she wondered if she'd run into him at work.

The hours were meant to give undergraduate students a chance to observe those experiencing psychological issues, so she could decide what area she wanted to specialize in after graduation. She knew she needed to get a master's degree, and there were other educational requirements if she continued on the path to becoming a psychologist. She tried not to think of the long road ahead to get her Ph.D. She'd already signed up for the master's program, so she could sign up for classes next semester if she continued.

She didn't have time to consider anything else until she was back outside in the sunshine. As she walked toward her car to go home for a quick lunch before work, she smiled.

She'd see Jason again Friday morning, but they weren't going to have much time to talk before class. She had her Special Topics in Psychology class right before Oral Communications and didn't have much time to get from one classroom to the other. She already regretted taking the Special Topics class. She didn't need the two credits. She'd signed up because the topic was sibling relationships, and her relationships with her brothers needed help.

She got home and prepared a lunch of chicken and carrot sticks before texting Jill. She and Jill could talk about it, and she'd get a clearer idea if she should drop the class or continue as planned. She didn't want to wait until her roommate got home for the evening.

"Met an interesting guy," she texted. She sat on the couch in her living room, her plate in her lap. If Jill was free at all, she'd respond to Ashley's provocative text.

Sure enough, as Ashley finished her meal, her cell rang.

"Where? Who?" Jill demanded.

Ashley laughed. "I figured you'd be calling."

"I need all the information, which can't be done by texting, now can it, girlfriend?" Jill asked.

"Well, it would be a rather lengthy text."

"Spill it. I'm eating lunch as we speak, and I only have a half hour."

"I went to the Oral Communications class. Still dreading it, by the way. I got there at the last minute because I was talking to someone, and time got away from me."

Jill laughed. "Why does that always happen to you? No, don't answer. Go on with the story."

"There were two desks left. One in the middle of the class where I would have to crawl over everyone, or one in the front row by this guy who was asleep."

"You took the one by the sleeping guy, I take it."

"Who's telling this story?" Ashley asked, but she smiled.

"You. Too slow. Time's passing."

"Then let me finish so you can go back to work, and I can get to my job. Anyway, the teacher came in and looked at the guy, and I got this sudden urge to wake him up, so maybe he'd avoid the wrath of the instructor. I poked him in the arm, and he jerked awake and looked around. Dr. Williams, the instructor, found it humorous and assured me, if Jason fell asleep again, I could repeat the jab."

"You know his name?" Jill asked.

Of course Jill would notice that piece of information. "We had a brief conversation in the hallway after class and exchanged names. I had to get to an appointment with my advisor."

"Is Jason cute?"

"Yeah, kind of. I mean he's not gorgeous or anything, but he is attractive. He's an older student too. I have reservations. Why was he sleeping? I hope it wasn't because of a hangover. You know I couldn't deal with that," Ashley said.

"Yeah. Because of your brother, but he's sober now, isn't he?" Jill asked.

"I think so." Her mind wandered to her brothers, whom she missed.

"Ashley? Are you there?" Jill asked.

"Sorry. I was remembering. I better let you go. I do need to talk to you about my brothers and that class, but your lunchtime is probably up by now. Thanks for listening."

"What are you going to do?"

Ashley laughed. "What do you think? I'm going to stay in the class, and we'll see what happens with everything. Jason will be my incentive since my class with him is right after the sibling class. We'll talk more when you get home this evening and have time."

"Good for you. I've heard Paul has a new girlfriend. Hannah works in fundraising at the hospital. She's probably a softening influence. It'll all work out. See you after work."

Hopefully Jill was right about Paul's attitude change, and time had softened his demeanor. Ashley hung up and looked around the room. Life was going to be interesting in the next few months.

Her brother, Alex, would be getting out of prison soon. The past would be raked up, and her sister-in-law could use support. Ashley always liked Courtney, but Courtney told her the best thing to do was stay away from them and not be tainted by Alex's actions.

Ashley shouldn't have listened to their advice, even if Courtney and Alex wanted her to stay far away. Because of it, she'd missed spending time with both of them since Alex went to prison for embezzlement. She regretted the missed time, as she could never get it back. She had to remind herself she was two years older now and knew more about life in general than she had back then.

CHAPTER 2

Jason got home in time for lunch. He walked into the kitchen and looked over his mother's shoulder as she stood holding a spoon over a pot. Chicken and dumplings. His favorite. He gave her a quick hug. "Looks good, Mom."

She patted his arm with her free hand. "Thanks."

"I'm going to change out of these school duds and into my farm clothes. Then I can help you with anything you need." He headed upstairs to his room, whistling tunelessly. He thought of Ashley. She was cute with her short curly dark hair. He'd been surprised when she woke him in class.

He'd never fallen asleep in class before, but they pushed hard on the farm to get harvest done, and he hadn't gotten a lot of sleep lately. It wouldn't happen again because he realized thinking of Ashley gave him energy. Sitting next to her would be the jolt he needed to keep awake during class.

He bounded down the stairs and into the kitchen. "What can I do?" he asked his mom.

She put a potholder in the center of the table, which was already set with dishes and silverware. "You can set the pot from the stove right here. I'll get the salad and dressing out of the fridge."

His sister, Madison, joined them in the kitchen. She carried Chloe, Jason's niece, who sucked on a pacifier. After he set the pan on the potholder on the table, he gently rubbed the side of Chloe's cheek. He saw the smile behind the pacifier. She lifted her arms to him, and he took her from Madison.

"Thanks," Madison said. "She's only a few months old, but it feels like she's gained a ton since her birth. I already fed her, so here." She handed Jason a towel for his shoulder. "She's been spitting up when she burps, so good luck."

He smiled at Chloe. "You wouldn't spit up all over your uncle, would you?"

He sat down at the table and shifted Chloe to one arm. His mom and Madison joined him. They said the blessing and started passing food back and forth. "Dad out in the field yet?" he asked.

"Yes. When you're done eating, he said he'd come in and eat."

"Sounds good. I appreciate he's letting me take this class. I have to take one class on campus every semester. I wish it wasn't right in the middle of the morning. At least the online classes are on my own time."

His mother waved her hand as if it were a magic wand. "You've put in so many hours helping here on the farm. Long past the time we expected to have help, so don't worry about it. You deserve to get your degree and move on with your life."

Jason didn't know why, but it made him feel guilty. When he finished his degree, he'd be leaving the farm instead of taking it over and letting his father retire. Maybe not right away, but eventually, depending on job possibilities. His parents supported whatever path he chose. Until now, he hadn't known what he wanted to do. Right now, they were all concentrating on Madison and little Chloe. He would do his part on the farm, plus help their neighbor Frank as much as possible. Then maybe when he got his associate degree, he'd be able to start his own business and take some electrician classes.

"You look far away. Did something happen in class?" Madison asked him.

Of course she would notice. He smiled. "Now don't get upset, Mom. Everything is okay. The teacher found it amusing."

His mom's hand, holding a forkful of chicken, paused on its way to her mouth before she continued the motion and went back to eating. "I'm sure it's fine if you say so."

He caught the doubt in her voice. "Don't worry. I fell asleep before class, and my classmate poked me awake in time for the lecture. Like I said, the teacher thought her jabbing me was funny."

Madison's eyes lit up. "Was the girl cute?"

Jason's face flushed, but he had a dark tan from working outside over the summer, so he hoped she didn't notice. "She was okay."

His sister stared at him and smiled as if she knew a secret. "Okay."

That was all she said but he knew she'd caught on that he found Ashley attractive.

His mother wasn't quite ready to drop the subject. "Are you sure the teacher was okay with it?"

"He's fine. Don't worry, Mom. It's not going to happen again."

She frowned. "You're trying to do too much. I knew it when you said you wanted to go to school. We should hire someone to help around the farm."

He mentally kicked himself for bringing up the story. It wasn't a disaster. "Mom, everything's fine. Harvest will be done tomorrow, and that's always a busy time. I won't be falling asleep again."

He got up and kissed the top of her head. "Don't worry. All's well. I need to get out to the field."

Madison got up to take Chloe from him.

"You finish lunch." Jason pointed Madison back to the table. "I'll lay her down on her blanket on the floor. She'll be fine for a few more minutes. I'll keep checking on her until I leave."

He spread Chloe's blanket and a few toys on the living room floor and laid a contented Chloe in the middle of it.

He started gathering what he needed to take to the field, checking on her every few minutes. She fought against sleep, and he smiled. Her lids would fall, and she forced them open.

He was ready after pulling out two bottles of water and a cola from the fridge. "She's all yours. She looks like she'll be asleep in a few minutes."

Madison scooped up the last of the food on her plate. "I should change her quickly then and let her sleep." She took her dishes to the sink. "I'll do dishes, Mom. Let me get Chloe settled first."

"Thanks, dear."

"See you later, Jason," Madison called from where she sat on the floor changing the baby.

He waved on his way out.

CHAPTER 3

Ashley spent the rest of the day interning at the mental health unit at St. Gertrude's Medical Center, so she had no time for thoughts of Jason or her brothers intruding at odd moments. During her first week at work, she concentrated on learning the rules and regulations of the hospital.

By the end of the day, she slouched on the couch after eating dinner. Her roommate, Jill, hadn't come home yet from her nursing job, so Ashley enjoyed the peace of having the place to herself. She liked these free moments in the evening. She got to relax for a short time before she started studying.

She searched the internet for the books she needed on sibling relationships and for her speech class on Friday and ordered them in both digital and paperback formats. She ordered the extra books too but just in digital format.

Thank goodness the Special Topics class only met for an hour on Monday and Friday. Oral Communications met Monday, Wednesday, and Friday. That might give her a chance to talk to Jason on Wednesday.

She looked at the first type of speech she needed to give. Informative. They had to give two informative speeches and two persuasive speeches total. There were also other types of speeches, although they didn't have to do anything vocal for them, just study them for exams.

Jill arrived home just as Ashley was going to open the digital book on speeches. She was happy to be interrupted.

"What are you reading?" Jill asked as she stepped out of her slip-on shoes. She left them in the entryway and padded into the kitchen.

The open floor plan gave Ashley a good look at Jill's frowning face as she pulled a spoon out of the drawer.

"I was just opening a book about speeches. Did something bad happen at work?" Ashley asked her.

"Just tired." Jill reached into the fridge and pulled out a yogurt. She closed the door. "It was a long shift. Short of other nurses to help, as usual. I wish we had a full staff."

"Do you want to sit and watch a movie or something?"

"I want to talk more about your classes and Jason." Jill took a seat on the recliner and lifted the footrest.

Ashley sprawled out on the couch across from her and set her tablet on the floor by the couch. "If it'll take your mind off work, I'm happy to discuss classes. I'm so conflicted about this semester. I can't believe I'm going to graduate in December with my bachelor's degree in psychology. I wanted to be a psychologist, but now I don't know. Maybe that's not what I want to do."

Jill stopped spooning up yogurt and stared at Ashley. "You what? After four years of studying, you're changing your mind? Didn't you have any idea before now that you were on the wrong track?"

Ashley sat up. "You believe I'm on the wrong track?"

"No. I was repeating what you said." She started eating again.

"I've still got a lot of school to go, and clinicals, and certification exams. And on and on. It suddenly doesn't feel like the right thing anymore." Ashley didn't know how to explain the uncertainty that she'd been feeling since summer. She knew she was going to at least get her bachelor's degree. After that—she didn't know.

"Are you just feeling overwhelmed? If you were done in December and could practice as a psychologist, would you feel the same way? Is it all the work needed yet?" Jill asked.

"No. I don't know why, but I've changed and don't think it's for me." She'd been lost for an answer for a while now.

"You must have gone into the program for some reason. Why did you want to become a psychologist in the first place?"

"I wanted to help people with dyslexia. I had a friend who got help with some of the newer treatments and ways of reading with dyslexia, and she was so excited. I guess I wanted to help people like her have a better life. I didn't want to specialize."

"Speech therapists and teachers can help once there's a diagnosis. Do either of those sound like something you want to do?" Jill asked.

"No."

They sat there silently for a while.

Jill finished her yogurt and set the container on the coffee table between them. "What does this Jason look like?"

Ashley smiled at her. "I wondered how long it would take you to get to that subject."

"Well, the future discussion isn't moving along, so I thought I'd see about this guy."

"He's got dark hair and brown eyes. He has a wonderful smile." She felt her own smile growing. "His name is all I know because we didn't have time to get better acquainted before I had to meet with my advisor."

"And you're going to see him in class for the whole semester. He might be a good resource to help you get over your fear of speaking."

Ashley blushed and cringed. She hadn't even considered that. "I can't give a speech in front of him. Oh, no. What am I going to do? I can't quit the class. It's required to graduate."

Jill laughed gently. "If he likes you, you can practice speeches together. It will help to have a friend in the classroom when you give the speech," she encouraged.

"I'd rather make a fool of myself in front of a bunch of strangers."

"Me too. People I won't ever see again. Anyway, what about your other class that discusses sibling relationships? Are you staying in that class?"

"Yes. I signed up because I want to figure out how to mend fences with my brothers. It's been two years since I talked to either one of them. We need to reunite. Now that Paul is alone since his wife and child died, he would probably like to get together again, even if he is dating. I'm hoping he wants to get together again. And Alex gets out of prison the first of December."

She didn't like the estrangement. The situation with both of them felt so complicated. Jason was interesting, and if she wanted a relationship with any guy, she needed to address her abandonment issues brought on by interactions she'd had with her parents and siblings. It had been a long time since she found a guy attractive.

"I want to drop the sibling class, but I'm hoping there will be information I learn to help my relationships with Paul and Alex."

Jill was quiet for a minute, and then she said softly, "You deliberately signed up because of the subject matter. That's a sign that you're on the right track, and it's time, Ashley. Maybe God wants you to try and mend your relationships with them."

"Maybe. There's a lot to forgive."

"There always is. Life isn't perfect. People aren't perfect. Maybe consider it?" Jill suggested.

"I'm thinking. Believe me, I'm thinking," Ashley said.

"Good. You saw Paul from a distance at the funeral. You made the first move."

"You're right. It was hard to attend, but he'd just lost his wife and daughter in a car accident. I needed to go no matter how difficult our relationship is. He smiled at me, like he was glad to see me. He didn't approach me. He left that up to me."

"He probably appreciated that you went to the funeral," Jill said.

"Probably." Ashley remembered the sweet smile on his face when he'd seen her. And deep down, she knew she missed him. She wanted Paul and Alex back in her life. They had great times growing up. And then life happened. She also missed Alex's wife, Courtney. If nothing else, she should have stood by her and helped her through the last few years. She felt guilty about not being there for her, even though that had been Courtney and Alex's choice, not hers.

Jill yawned and got up. She picked up her yogurt container. "I'm going to read in bed for a while."

"You'll probably fall asleep before you get a page read."

"Probably." She went into the kitchen and threw away the container. Before she started walking down the hallway to the bedroom, she stopped at the foot of the couch. "If you want to talk more about the future and school, let me know. Just think about what you want to do, and what you like to do. You'll come up with your answer."

Ashley looked down at her hands twisting in her lap. She'd been thinking about it for months and hadn't come up with an idea. She had four months to arrive at an answer. Sooner would be better. She yelled toward where Jill had disappeared down the hallway, "And, by the way, I know you. Something happened at work. When you're ready, I'm here to listen to you too."

#

Friday, she woke up half nervous and half excited to see Jason again. First she had to get through her Special Topics in Psychology class on sibling relationships.

Dr. Athena moved to the center of the room. "I see we lost a few classmates from last time. I'm assuming the rest of you are here because the subject is of interest to you, or you couldn't find another class to replace this one." Her eyes twinkled.

Ashley wanted to stand up and say, "Not me. I want to know everything about siblings."

"You had the assignment on Wednesday and a chance to get the books needed for the class. I'm sure there are a few of you who have read the readings, and a few of you who haven't."

The class laughed.

"Just a reminder that we will only be meeting on Fridays and Mondays from now on. When we met on Wednesday, it was to replace the day before Thanksgiving. For today's class, you'll be given a reprieve if you haven't read the assignment but don't expect a repeat. I'm guessing there may be a few in the class who don't have any siblings. Please raise your hand if you don't have any?"

Four people raised their hands.

"Thank you. You can lower your hands. I assume the rest of the class has siblings. I believe you'll find, even if you didn't grow up with siblings, parts of this class may pertain to your other relationships, such as friendships. Especially if you have a large group of friends. If that's not the case, don't worry. You won't be graded on how applicable the subject of siblings is to your life.

"I'll be assigning four papers for you to write. Your grade will be based on those papers. Today's topic is birth order and how that affects our choices in life. I gave you the first chapter to read for class today. Who wants to volunteer where they are in birth order in their family and how it has affected you?" Dr. Athena asked.

There was a pause, and then a young woman raised her hand. She looked to be about twenty, and Ashley was impressed by the number of piercings in her nose. "I'm in the middle of a family of six. I'm the peacemaker. Sometimes I hate that position. I feel like I get lost in the middle of everything. My parents love us all, but I'm not the oldest, and I'm not the youngest, and they seem to get the most attention." She suddenly flushed red.

Then she lifted her head proudly. "I guess that shows how jealous I am of them at times, but I usually get along with them."

"Thank you for sharing your experience," Dr. Athena said. "That is a common phenomenon in families. There's usually a favorite or two in a large family. Parents are people, which we forget. They have their own personalities and mesh better with some of their children. That doesn't mean they don't love us. It means their relationship may be smoother and appear to have less angst with it."

A young guy in a blue hoodie and jeans raised his hand. His dark hair had enough curls in it to make it a little ruffled. His brown eyes were serious. "I'm the oldest in a family with three children. Do I think I'm my parents' favorite? Well, my mother's favorite. Not so much my dad's. We don't agree with each other on a lot of things, but my mother would probably do anything for me.

"It makes me feel guilty. Like I don't deserve her love. I mean, I make mistakes, but instead of telling her something she should know, I feel like I have to hide it, or she won't love me anymore. She's blinded by love sometimes, but my dad can see when I've done something wrong. He probably can read my emotions better because he doesn't love me like my mom does."

He paused. "I guess that didn't come out right. My dad loves me, just not with the closed-eye love like Mom."

Dr. Athena nodded. "That's another complication in sibling relationships and in parent-child relationships. Gender plays a part too. Birth order doesn't always affect the way a family operates. A child can connect with a parent because of habits or hobbies in common. A lack of things in common doesn't doom a relationship, however. In fact, it doesn't matter if a parent and child have anything in common or not. It's more dependent on if they accept their differences, but realize they're in the same family, and that's enough."

"One thing I want to emphasize while we're discussing this subject. Because someone doesn't fit into the general mold we're discussing doesn't mean there's anything wrong with them. We're all different. Even if ten of you are from a family of three, there will be all manner of differences in how your family may look. Please remember, we're generalizing here, so don't go home and feel like something's wrong with you because your situation is different. Different makes the world go around. What if we were all alike? How boring for us all.

"Thank you all for participating. You have the assignment for next Monday. Also, a reminder about Monday for those of you who haven't read the syllabus. Bring paper and a pen or pencil on Monday. You'll be writing a short essay during class. I will be bringing a paper shredder in case you decide you don't want to take the paper with you and want it destroyed. I know. Old-school.

"Class dismissed."

#

Ashley made it to her next class about five minutes early, as the class right before hers ended. She saw Jason standing in the hallway along with a few other early arrivals. She went over to him. He looked cute in his worn jeans and short-sleeved black t-shirt.

"Hi," he said. "I'm awake this time."

She laughed. "It's hard to take a nap in the hallway, especially when another class is charging out of the classroom."

By that time, the classroom had emptied. They followed the other students who had been standing in the hallway into the room. Jason sat in the same seat he had on Wednesday. Ashley sat next to him again.

He pulled his notebook and the speech book out of his backpack, and then turned to her. "First, thanks for getting me out of trouble last class. I can't believe I fell asleep."

"Oh, it was nothing. A spur-of-the-moment impulse on my part. Dr. Williams focused on you. Before I knew it, my finger flew out, and you were awake."

"All by itself?" He smiled.

"All by itself." She returned his smile. He had a nice one. "How come you were asleep anyway? You don't look like the partying type."

He took a deep breath and let it out. "I'm not. I work on a farm, and we were working long hours to get the harvest in. When I finally sat down, I guess I drifted off."

"You look more rested today." She cringed when she said it. "Sorry. That came out wrong."

He laughed. "I know what you mean. We're finished with getting the grain out of the field. Now it's a matter of repairs and catching up on everything else. At least we don't have to worry about the weather anymore. We can move slower and get more rest."

"It must be hard to run a farm and go to school. You said 'we.' Who does that include?"

"My father and me. We have a small farm, and we help our neighbor, Frank. He's got fewer acres. I think he's getting ready to retire."

"Do you have any siblings?" Ashley asked as Dr. Williams came into the classroom.

"One younger sister. You?"

"Two brothers." She was relieved that class was about to start because she didn't have time to discuss her brothers right now. "Looks like Dr. Williams is about ready."

"Do you want to meet for coffee sometime?" Jason asked.

"I'd like that." Her heart beat a little faster at the idea of getting to know him better.

He handed her a piece of paper. "Here's my phone number. Text if you want to set something up. I guess we better pay attention to the instructor now." He flashed her another smile and then faced forward.

Ashley tucked the piece of paper with the number into her jeans pocket. The ten minutes before class had passed quickly.

Next up, Dr. Williams. She was nervous during the class as she anticipated seeing Jason again sometime for coffee and having to give a speech.

She wasn't sure what he meant by writing his phone number down before they'd even gotten into the classroom. Did women fall all over themselves for him all the time? She'd find out more when they had coffee.

Ashley looked at her watch. 10:50 a.m. The time had passed quickly. She didn't realize they were there for the full class. She assumed Dr. Williams dismissed them early. She'd even managed to ignore Jason part of the time.

He gathered up his things. "Well, I'm done with classes for the day. How about you?"

"I have to work at one o'clock, but I'm free until then."

"Want to get an early lunch?" He stood there with his backpack over his shoulder and his arms crossed, as if waiting for a rejection.

Wow. Her heartbeat fluttered crazily. They were having lunch with their coffee now? Jason had surprised her, but it only took her a moment to respond. "Sounds good. I have to eat before work anyway. Did you have a specific place in mind?"

He dropped his arms to his sides and smiled. "There's a burger place a few blocks away. They have salads too, if you prefer."

"Sure. It's nice outside. It was somewhere around sixty-eight degrees right before class started. Do you want to walk?"

"Sure." She gathered her folder and notebook and stuck them in her backpack where her tablet and purse already resided.

They headed out of the building, into the sunshine. Suddenly Ashley couldn't think of a thing to say, and either Jason had the same problem or didn't feel the need for conversation.

She looked at him out of the corner of her eye. He smiled as he walked and didn't seem concerned about the silence. "What did you think of class today?" she asked.

He looked over at her. "It's interesting, isn't it? I have to admit, I'm nervous about speaking in front of everyone."

She was surprised and relieved. She wasn't the only person scared to get up in front of everyone. "I would never have guessed that. You come across as very self-assured and calm. No one would know you aren't. Unfortunately, I turn beet red, and there's no hiding the fact that I'm scared stiff."

"Would you like to get together and practice our speeches with each other?" he asked.

"That sounds like a good idea. I can have you and Jill critique them for me."

"Who is Jill?"

"My friend and roommate. We've known each other since I moved to Bismarck." She didn't have time to get into the complicated situation with her youth, so she changed the subject. Since family was on her mind, she'd ask about his. "Tell me about your sister."

"We get along great. She's a lot younger than me. I'm twenty-nine, and she's turning eighteen soon. I got to be her babysitter when Mom and Dad had things to do, which happened often when she was a baby. I was twelve when she was born."

"Wow. That's a big difference. I have two older brothers, Alex and Paul." She quickly changed the subject back to him. "What was it like living on a farm?"

"I did chores around the farm. Of course, Dad and Mom did any driving when it came to fieldwork. I was about fourteen when they let me run the tractor around the field for simple things."

"That sounds young." Ashley pictured a fourteen-year-old Jason, listening to music as he circled a field in a tractor. She didn't have much experience with farm life. She'd lived in Chokecherry Valley off and on, but their house was on the edge of town, and she hadn't had any friends. Her parents weren't farmers. They had family money. She'd spent most of her high school years in Bismarck, staying with her grandmother while her parents jetted around the world. "Where is the farm located?"

"The farm is just outside Chokecherry Valley. I live with my parents and my sister, Madison, and her daughter, Chloe. It's busy out there. Do you know where Chokecherry Valley is?"

"Yes. I grew up there until I turned thirteen. Maybe you know my brothers. They went to high school around there, but I stayed in Bismarck with my grandmother. Paul and Alex Richmond?" Ashley remembered the few times she'd been out to visit Paul's in-laws who lived outside of town by Chokecherry Valley. "My brother Paul's parents-in-law live on a farm out in Chokecherry Valley too. Frank and Nina."

"Oh, they're our neighbors. Your brothers are Paul and Alex? I know you mentioned them, but I didn't put it together," Jason said. "I know Paul, mostly from the summer planting season this year when he helped Frank and Nina. They're our next-door neighbors in the country. I know Alex too, as he was a year younger than me at school. And, of course, I saw him around town, until—"

"Until Alex went to jail." She knew the moment he said he was from Chokecherry Valley that he would know what happened with her brother. It was a small town. Ashley knew Paul stayed close to Frank and Nina's farm when he'd worked there over the spring and summer. She hadn't realized Jason's family were their neighbors.

"Right. We don't need to talk about Alex right now," he said easily, as if he were dismissing the weather as a subject. "It helped having Paul there during the spring planting season this year. There's a lot to do, and my parents and Nina and

Frank aren't getting any younger. I work for Frank when Paul isn't there."

"That must keep you busy."

"Yes, it does." He stopped in front of the burger place. "Here we are. Are you hungry?"

"Very hungry. I only ate a banana for breakfast. I was in a hurry." She didn't tell him she always rushed around in the mornings. She dragged herself out of bed, and then always ran out of time before she needed to leave the house.

They seated themselves at a small booth in the red-and-white-checked deco restaurant. Ashley didn't even scan the menu, leaving it where the server placed it. She knew what she wanted. She noticed Jason didn't look either.

"Do you know what you want?" Ashley asked him.

He nodded. "I come here a lot. If I have time between classes, this is where I go."

Ashley looked around at the classic diner. There were booths around the perimeter and tables in the center of the room. All of them were covered with red-and-white-checkered tablecloths. Black-and-white pictures hung on the walls.

The waitress came and took their order. A Reuben sandwich for Jason, and a hamburger and fries for Ashley.

"I kind of pictured you as a salad person," Jason said.

Ashley laughed. "I eat my vegetables. Usually. I need protein to get through the rest of the afternoon, and, I'll be honest, a potato in any form is my favorite food."

He had a nice laugh. Soft and low. "What about you? We've talked about my farm work, and you know I go to school. What keeps you busy?"

The waitress set their drinks on the table and left.

Ashley took a sip of her water. "I'm a senior. I'll graduate at the end of December because I took a few extra classes in the past few years to graduate a semester early. I was going to become a psychologist, so my major is psychology. I'm thinking about changing my career path. I'm not sure if I want to become a psychologist. In the afternoons, I have a clinical observation class at St. Gertrude's Medical Center for a few weeks to see what the work would be like."

"That should help you decide if you want to continue studying psychology, shouldn't it?"

"I hope so. I feel directionless now. Is that even a word?" She laughed to lighten the mood. "Enough about me. You sound busy with farmwork and school."

Jason shrugged. "I'm used to it, and I love farmwork."

"What's your major?"

"I'm just starting an associate degree. As much as I love farming, there's not a lot of money in small farms. School won't be as difficult to fit into my schedule during winter. There's not as much to do on the farm. We have a few cattle, and you can't do fieldwork in frozen ground covered by snow. Spring might be complicated, but we can hire someone to help for a short time. Fortunately, this degree is a two-year program. I only have to take a few general classes, like this speech class and an

English class. Otherwise, the classes all pertain to business. I'd like to be an electrician, but I want to have the business degree first. Then I'll probably get an electrician's certification."

Their food arrived while Jason talked, and Ashley dug into her burger immediately. Time passed quickly, and she was going to have to eat and run like usual to get to the hospital. "It sounds like a good fit, if it's what you're interested in doing."

Jason took a bite of his food, chewed, and swallowed before he answered, "I'm more excited by the electrician part, but business knowledge is necessary." He grinned wryly. "Besides, it will come in useful no matter what happens."

"Sorry I'm eating fast, but I've got to get going," Ashley told him.

"Don't worry. We can meet up again." His cheeks reddened, and he paused. "I mean, if you're interested?"

She'd heard the question at the end of his sentence, so she stuck a fry in her mouth to give herself time. Did she want to get together with Jason? She wasn't experienced in relationships with guys. Should she tell him? Or let things happen as they happened?

She liked Jason, and he seemed nice. He was worth the time to see if they could be friends. "Sure. I'd like that."

"Great," he said. "I guess it's time for us to get going."

"Yes. You have to get back to the farm, and I have to get to the hospital." She felt let down at the idea of leaving. She reminded herself she'd see him in class, and they agreed to get together again. She wanted to see where the situation went.

Ashley and Jason walked to her car first. When he saw her safely inside the driver's seat, he left for his own vehicle. Ashley drove home and quickly changed into her work clothes, a light blue sweater and a pair of navy pants and blue loafers. She'd noticed it was generally cold in the counseling rooms in the afternoon, despite the weather being warm for September. Maybe because they were on the north side of the building.

By the time she arrived at work, she had little time to get from the parking lot to the office. She glanced at her phone.

Jill had texted, "How was class?" with added red heart emojis. She was for sure going to push a relationship with Jason.

Ashley texted back, "Great. Class was good. Lunch with Jason. Just walking into the office for work. Want delivery pizza after work? If yes, text me when you're ready to leave work, and I'll order it. I know I'll be done before you. Gotta go!"

She put the phone on silent and stuck it in her pocket as she went in to meet with her supervisor to talk through the afternoon schedule of patients.

CHAPTER 4

Ashley looked at the phone as it rang. She'd been busy cleaning the apartment while Jill worked all weekend. Why was Paul calling her? They hadn't talked for years. Not since he told her to leave his house and never come back. He and Samantha were drunk at the time.

She let it go to voicemail. It looked like God was trying to tell her the time had come to put the past behind her, to forgive her brothers and have an adult relationship with them. Otherwise, why would He have given her the urge to sign up for a class about siblings, and now Paul was calling her out of the blue?

She listened to his voicemail.

"I can understand why you probably don't want to talk with me. It won't help my case to say I was plastered that night. I only remember bits and pieces. That was my life before I got sober. I've been sober now for two years, and I'd like to repair our relationship, or start over, or whatever you want. Please give me a call if you can find it in your heart to talk to me," Paul said. The voicemail clicked off.

She sank down on the couch with the feather duster in one hand and her phone in the other. When she realized she was gripping them, she set them both on the coffee table and leaned back onto the couch cushions.

It was good to hear from Paul. He sounded like the older brother she knew before alcohol took over his life. She felt like crying. She knew when the class she signed up for involved the topic of siblings, she was ready to connect with one or both of her brothers. She believed it would be in her time frame. The moment had come, but she wasn't as ready as she'd hoped.

She needed someone to talk to about all of it. Jill wouldn't be available until after work, which was hours away. Maybe Jason would have time. She had no idea what he'd planned for today, other than working on the farm. And why would he come to mind? She'd only met him a few days ago.

She should call Paul and talk to him. She sat there, not making a move to call him back. What if she called him, and then it all fell apart again? Could she handle that? She was older and stronger mentally now. Yes, she could handle it. She'd take it slow.

Right now, she needed to calm down. She got her camera to take pictures. That always took her mind off her problems. There were lovely autumn trees with gorgeous colors she noticed when driving to work and school. The leaves wouldn't stay on the trees much longer.

She put away her cleaning supplies, ate a tuna sandwich, and drank a glass of water. After changing into jeans and a bright yellow t-shirt, she gathered her camera and a couple of bottles of water and left the apartment.

She drove to a park she'd noticed yesterday near her apartment. Today was Saturday, and parents brought their kids to the parks on the weekend, so she didn't expect it to be as quiet as yesterday. She was right. Fortunately, the trees were on the opposite side of the park from the playground equipment. She could take pictures without constant questions from the children and querying looks from parents.

A lovely maple in a glorious red shade glinted in the sun, and she focused mostly on that tree. Then she moved on to other yellow and gold trees. After that, she backed away and did wide panoramas of large sections of the trees.

She felt calmer after taking the pictures, and when she returned to her car, she decided to phone Paul right then. Parked at the curb with the trees between her and the playground, it would be hard for anyone to see what she did. Not that there was anything wrong with it. She was always paranoid at playgrounds after one mother accused her of taking pictures of her daughter—which she hadn't been doing.

One of the curvy slides was beautiful, and she'd been considering how it would make a good background for a picture. She hadn't even noticed the girl, who had been playing on the swing a distance away. Fortunately, they were the only ones at the park when the mother started screaming at her to leave the playground, or she'd call the police.

Putting the memory aside, she set her camera on the passenger seat and pulled her phone out of her back pocket. Before she talked herself out of it, she pushed the return call button for Paul on her phone and listened to it ring.

"Hello," he answered.

"Hi, Paul. It's Ashley." Her voice shook slightly, and she clenched her free hand into a fist.

"Thanks so much for calling me back. It means a lot to me. As I said in my message, I'm sorry for the things I said, and I don't expect forgiveness, but I have to try."

His eager voice sounded sincere. "Why now, Paul? I mean, it's been a few years since our fight. Why do you want to talk now?"

"It's time. One of us has to take the first step. You were gracious enough to come to the funeral. It meant everything to me to see you there. I was so alone when they died."

"Is that why you're calling me now?" Annoyance crept into her voice. "Because you're alone?" She felt bad for him, but she wasn't going to fill some hole in his life after what he said to her.

"No. No." She heard him take a deep breath.

"I'm not alone," he said. "I have Frank and Nina, Hannah, and other friends. I'm doing fine, and I realized I needed to make amends to you and Alex. And I want you in my life too. I know this is a lot to take in, but we're family. Our parents dumped us, and we didn't know what to do. Now, it's time to take a look at our family and try and salvage what we can. Family is important."

Family is important, she repeated to herself silently. It would be nice to be a family with Alex and Paul again. If they were like they were when they were growing up. Not if they were going to be the adult versions she'd known. She hoped they'd both grown up since their experiences.

"Are you there?" Paul asked.

"Yes. I was remembering when we were younger." She heard the wistfulness in her voice. "We three took care of each other while Mom and Dad traveled around the world."

"Until I started drinking and partying in high school. You went to stay with Grandma," Paul said. "I'm sorry. I'm not proud of how I behaved. I feel maybe that led to what Alex did. If I had been paying attention, maybe he would have come to me and asked for help."

She felt compelled to dispute his idea for some reason. "Alex was a grown man. He was twenty-seven and knew what he was doing was wrong. You can't take the blame."

"He'll need help now. He and Courtney both will. I plan to approach him when he's out of jail. I don't know what he thinks either, since he continually told me not to visit him in prison or go see Courtney," he explained. "Would you consider getting together to talk? I'd like to see you again."

"I was hurt, Paul. I'm going to have to think about this and pray." She wanted to see him, but she was suddenly afraid of additional hurt, so she backed out of immediately saying yes. "I will say it's likely I'll get together with you, but I need time to adjust now that we've talked. I'll give you a call when I'm ready."

"Thank you. I appreciate it. I'll wait to hear from you. Bye, Ashley."

She pushed the end button with a sweaty finger. The part of her heart that tightened whenever she started getting close to someone loosened its grip. Would reuniting with Paul and Alex open her heart to other relationships?

CHAPTER 5

Amy stroked Baby Chloe's cheek where the tears leaked from her eyes as she lay in the crib. After a few minutes, Chloe quit crying and stared at Amy, fascinated by the light surrounding the seven-year-old.

Amy knew that light came from God because she'd come down from Heaven to comfort the child. For some reason, God had sent her to this baby. She must have something to do with Amy's father, Paul, who still lived on Earth. Whenever someone from her dad or her mother's family needed help, God would send Amy or her mother, Samantha, from Heaven to help them.

Amy whispered, "You're okay. See? There's nothing to cry about. I'm here, and God's here. We'll take care of you."

There might have been a smile on the baby's face behind her pacifier. She settled down and quit crying.

Amy kept stroking her face and then her arm. She could hear Madison crying outside, and then a vehicle drove up the gravel road. She knew it was time to leave. Someone else had come to help Chloe.

Amy heard the baby start crying when she disappeared, but she knew it would only be a few minutes before someone took care of her again.

CHAPTER 6

Jason arrived home at his parents' farm in Chokecherry Valley to find his sister sitting on the top step of the house sobbing hysterically. He jumped out of his vehicle and ran to her. "What's wrong?"

"It's Chloe." She sniffled, swiped her nose with a tissue, then started sobbing again. "She wouldn't stop crying."

"Are Mom or Dad home?"

"No. They left for a while."

Jason cringed. "You left her alone in the house?"

He didn't wait for an answer and ran into the house. The minute he opened the front door, he heard Chloe crying. He had no idea how long they'd both been crying. This was not good.

He picked the baby up from her crib, crooning to her as he gently swayed, "Shh. It's okay. It's okay, Chloe."

She hiccupped a few times, and then sighed. She looked up at him in a sleepy way. Her lashes were wet, and she had a snotty nose. He found a tissue and wiped her nose gently to keep her from starting to cry again. He walked slowly into the kitchen, swaying and murmuring quietly to her. He found a bottle in the fridge and warmed it up in the microwave.

At least he knew how to do all this. He'd babysat Chloe often enough to know where to find everything and how to take care of her. When he gathered what he needed, he took Chloe into her bedroom and sat in the rocker, holding her.

She latched on to the bottle and sucked greedily as Jason gently rocked. He leaned back against the headrest and closed his eyes. What happened? He was concerned about Madison, but Chloe came first. He would talk to Madison when he settled the baby in her crib after she'd eaten and fallen asleep.

Madison had been having a hard time in the past few months since Chloe was born. He didn't remember a time when it had been this bad. He said a prayer for Chloe and Madison: *God, please let me know what to say and what to do to help this situation.*

He hadn't been praying enough lately, and it looked like things around him were starting to fall apart. It shouldn't take bad things happening before he prayed, but sometimes he lapsed without the reminder he needed God.

When Chloe finished the bottle, he burped her, changed her diaper, and walked around her room, swaying again. She looked up at him with her adorable brown baby eyes, and he was smitten. Had been since the first day he'd held her. She didn't look like she planned to sleep any time soon. She must have already napped.

He looked at the clock hanging on the wall, a simple pink plastic frame around the digits. 2:00 p.m. It didn't tell him anything of Chloe's schedule from the morning until now. He would ask Madison to come into the house, and he'd talk to her while he held Chloe.

He hadn't heard Madison crying since he came into the house, so maybe she'd gotten herself somewhat together. He walked over to the outside door and opened it. He leaned against it, keeping it open. Madison looked up from where she sat twisting her tissues in her hands.

Her look of relief hit him in the stomach. Something needed to be done. He didn't want to be the one to do it, but Madison listened to him more than she did to their parents. A teenager thing, he knew.

"You got her to stop crying. Thank you. I didn't know what to do anymore. The counselor said…"

A wary look passed through her eyes as she stopped talking, and he was afraid he knew where this was going. Madison had been seeing a counselor since Chloe's birth, and the rest of the family went along to one of the sessions to be given information about her diagnosis.

The counselor explained postpartum depression to them, and what Madison should do in certain circumstances. Their family tried not to leave her alone with the baby, but obviously something happened, and their parents had to leave.

"Let's go in the house and get comfortable. I'll take care of Chloe for a while." He kept leaning against the door until Madison came inside.

She went into the living room and sat with her feet curled beneath her on the couch. A pink bunny-patterned blanket covered the floor, and a few toys lay scattered on the soft surface.

Jason grabbed a soft gray stuffed elephant from the floor and settled in the recliner with Chloe.

"She needs to eat," Madison said quietly, picking at her fingernail polish and avoiding Jason's gaze.

Jason gathered his patience and spoke evenly, "I've fed her, changed her, and she's okay. What about you?"

"You hate me, don't you? I'm a bad mother." She blinked rapidly.

He sensed another bout of weeping, which he didn't want to deal with. He leaned forward in the recliner, keeping Chloe comfortably in front of him. "I don't hate you," he said softly. "I love you as much as I love Chloe. We need to talk about today and what to do."

As his last words registered, she looked up. "You love me?"

He smiled at her. "Of course. This is a tough time for you. You feel unlovable, and it doesn't help that Chloe's father took off and left you to take care of her alone."

"Alone, except for you and Mom and Dad."

"Where are Mom and Dad?"

"They went into Chokecherry Valley to help someone who broke her hip. She needed a ride."

Jason realized they'd need two people to help her.

"I was okay alone."

He almost laughed at the irony but kept his mouth shut. Sure, she was okay. That was why he came home to mayhem.

"Okay," she said. "It didn't last. She wouldn't quit crying, and I panicked. I left her in her crib and went outside. That's what the counselor told me to do if I felt like I couldn't deal with her calmly. I was afraid I'd drop her or something. I was crying as hard as her. I hoped if I put her in her crib, she might quit crying."

"How long ago did all this happen?" He worried about what they were going to do about this situation.

"About a half hour. When I went outside, she quit crying within a few minutes. I believed I could get it together enough to go in and feed her. Every time I got up to go inside, I'd remember what a bad mother I was and start crying again. She seemed okay. I only heard her start crying again when you drove up the driveway."

He rested against the back of the recliner again, trying to appear relaxed. "I'm going to say something, and I want you to listen to me, Madison. I know it's going to make you mad, but I think you know more needs to be done. This can't happen again."

"I know. I don't know what to do." Madison started picking at her fingernails again and sniffling. A box of tissues sat on the end table beside her, and she grabbed a few.

"You've gone over the scenarios with the counselor. You know what your choices are."

She nodded, wiped her nose, and sat up. She made direct eye contact with him for the first time since he'd arrived. "You're right. I'm her mother. I need to do what's best for her. The counselor doesn't know how long this depression will last, and I hoped I'd be fine by now. I'm not. I trust you, Jason, or I wouldn't say this.

"I've thought about giving her up for adoption again, but I can't take that step. And I know it would be a permanent solution to what is going to be a short-term problem. I know when I say short-term, it could be six months. In the scheme of things, six months isn't long compared to her entire childhood. I've decided to start medication."

"When did you decide to do that? I don't want you to make a rash decision, and then when we get to the doctor's office, you change your mind." She'd already done that several times in the past two months they'd been dealing with this.

"I'm not changing my mind this time. Chloe is my responsibility. I need to be here for her. I wasn't today, and none of the rest of you were either." She held up her hand when he started to speak.

"That's not an accusation. That's life. Things come up. I don't blame anyone except myself. I should have started on medication right away. I kept telling myself, tomorrow I'll be fine. And then I'd wake up the next day, and I wasn't fine. I'd think, okay, this will be slow, but I'll see progress. I'm not seeing any progress in getting better. I believed taking pills made me a weak person, but it doesn't. Postpartum depression is a disease like any other disease. It needs treatment," she said.

"I'm proud of you for considering all of this," Jason said, getting up from the recliner. He knelt in front of Madison with Chloe nestled in his left arm and gave his sister a hug with his right arm. "You'll get through this. I know you will."

She hugged him back, being careful not to squish Chloe between them. "Thank you. You've been a rock. I couldn't have done this without your help."

"You're welcome, anytime. Next time, try and remember to call me. Promise?"

"I promise." She smiled. It was brief, but it was there.

"Okay." He got up.

"Can I hold Chloe?" she asked tentatively.

"Of course." He handed the baby over to Madison. "Have you eaten lunch yet?"

"No." She played with Chloe's fingers, and the baby cooed.

"I'll get you something. Food will help you feel better too."

He went into the kitchen to get her a sandwich, hoping the conversation would be a turning point. He was sorry it took a total meltdown, and no one to help her, but the ending turned out okay. Thank goodness. Thank you, God.

CHAPTER 7

Ashley joined Jill on the couch that evening where they set out a pepperoni pizza and soft drinks for dinner. They planned on watching a movie, but Jill's questioning about Jason hindered making a movie choice.

"Are you two dating?" Jill asked.

"I wouldn't call it dating. We ate lunch together after class today. That's not a date, is it?" Ashley liked Jason, but she couldn't convince herself their lunch constituted a date. It was a spur-of-the-moment idea, and she'd been hungry. And he was cute. Maybe it was a date. Especially since they'd agreed to meet for lunch after class again.

Jill turned to look at her. "What would you do if he asked you out?"

"I don't know." She got up and escaped to the kitchen area, which was part of the open floor plan, to get more napkins. They were out, so she grabbed the pen off the counter and wrote "napkins" on the grocery list posted on the fridge.

She searched for the paper towels and finally found them in one of the cabinets. She tore a few off the roll as she walked back into the living room area.

Jill's gaze remained focused on her.

Ashley couldn't escape this inquisition. The whole subject made her nervous. "I plan on going out with him on a date. There. Are you happy?" She placed the towels on the coffee table with their dinner and put her hands on her hips.

Jill grinned. "Ecstatic."

"I have work and school to finish. Then I need to figure out if I'm continuing with school or finding a job. With only an undergraduate degree in psychology, my options in that field are limited. Most jobs in the field require a master's degree at minimum, plus certifications. I don't have time for a man, but I'll make time if Jason is interested. Now, let's choose a movie and eat. I'm starving."

She grabbed one of the two plates and put a slice of pizza on it. Then she grabbed her soda, popped the top and took a long drink. As she took a bite of pizza, she ignored Jill's stare. Next, she took the remote and changed the channel to a cozy mystery movie she knew Jill would find interesting.

Jill started getting her own dinner. "You know, you're going to have to deal with your past eventually. Not everyone is like your brothers. Or your parents."

"A recovered alcoholic and an embezzler. They're great examples. Oh, and my parents basically deserted us when we were growing up, leaving us with whoever would take us, while they traveled around the world."

"Well, Paul is sober now, right? He got his act together, and he told you he's been sober for two years. He didn't go back to drinking despite his wife and daughter's deaths. You have to give him credit for that. He's dating Hannah, who is wonderful," Jill said.

"I forgot you would know Hannah from the hospital."

"I don't know her. She hasn't done fundraising for our unit, but other people say she's great. Your brother did give a speech at the fundraiser for the NICU and impressed a lot of people."

"So, he got it together. Although we had a brief conversation, we aren't talking regularly yet. I know it looks like Paul and I are on track to being closer, but underneath my desire to reconcile, I am still so mad at him. I can't seem to get over the anger and hurt."

"Well, maybe this class will help you to mend fences. And Alex is getting out of jail soon. He'll probably need your support, along with his wife. Everyone makes mistakes. Aren't there things about your life you regret?" Jill paused and ate a few bites. "Weren't there any good times with your brothers when you were kids?"

Ashley remembered how her brothers stood up for her in school when someone teased her. That had mostly been Paul because Alex was oblivious. They stuck together at whoever's house their parents dumped them at when they traveled.

"There were good times. I'm hopeful this class will help me navigate a new relationship with them. I admit it. I am trying. With my brothers and with Jason. I'm so used to closing myself off in case I get hurt that it's hard to change old habits." She smiled at Jill. "Now let's eat and enjoy our pizza. It's getting cold."

"Glad you're making up with your brothers. And at least you're trying with Jason. When you have your first real date with him, you will let me know, won't you?" She grinned at Ashley.

"Funny." Ashley smiled at her and turned up the volume of the television slightly to hear over her own chewing. The subject was over for now with Jill, but it would come up again. She didn't want to think about Jason or her brothers any more this evening. She wanted to sink herself into watching the movie and forget her fear of rejection and hurt for a few hours. She was dealing with her feelings as much as she could, but the day had been emotional. She needed a break.

CHAPTER 8

Jason studied while waiting for his parents to return. When he'd finished making lunch for Madison, he suggested she take a nap. Then he called their neighbor Nina to see if she could babysit Chloe.

Nina was more than happy to take the baby for a few hours, so he loaded up the diaper bag with everything she might need. He peeked in at Madison, who had fallen into an exhausted sleep. He left a note for her in case she woke while he was gone.

Once he left Chloe with Nina, he returned home, changed into his work clothes, and did the chores on the farm. He picked up Chloe and now sat at the table studying.

Madison continued sleeping. That concerned him. She was either sleep-deprived or oversleeping. She needed to get on postpartum medication sooner rather than later, and he planned to discuss it with his parents when they returned. The therapist already suggested it, but Madison hadn't wanted to go on any medication. Her change of heart might be temporary, even after today's events. They needed to call the clinic and get the medication before she changed her mind.

He realized her mood swings made it hard for her to make an informed decision, but maybe with the support of the whole family, she would now take meds. She'd tried to deal with the depression for the two months since Chloe was born. That should be long enough to know medication was necessary.

He needed to remember it was her body and her choice, even if he didn't always agree with her decision. His would stand by her, help her take care of Chloe and wait it out.

Today showed him she couldn't be left alone with Chloe any longer until she recovered. The coordination of the effort to help would take everyone's time. With the harvest over, and the farmwork not as busy, it would be possible to focus on Madison.

His father arrived home, and Jason only had time to greet him before Madison came out of her bedroom.

She still looked half asleep, but her face muscles seemed more relaxed, and her eyes were clear. "Where's Mom?"

Their dad plopped down on the recliner in the living room and tossed a smile in Chloe's direction, and the baby quietly sucked on her finger as she lay on the blanket in the middle of the floor. "Your mom stayed at the hospital. The lady who fell didn't have any relatives or other friends who could stay with her, so your mom said she'd stay overnight until the lady's daughter arrived in the morning."

Jason's talk with his parents about Madison looked like it would be a conversation with his dad, him, and Madison. One phone call would be necessary to get the prescription anyway.

CHAPTER 9

Ashley started the homework due on Friday for her sibling class. Monday would be Labor Day, so there were no classes.

According to the instructions Dr. Athena gave them, they were to write three letters. One of the letters would be from her perspective to a sibling, and one would be from her sibling's perspective to her. The third letter excluded all the assumptions the other two letters contained, to boil it down to facts instead of assuming what the other person meant. She wasn't sure if it would be easier to write to Paul or Alex, but she chose Paul.

Dr. Athena promised not to share the letters in class without permission. She didn't plan to let her letters be read out loud.

Dear Paul,

I haven't talked to you in a long time, except for that brief phone call. I was hurt by the things you said in the past. As my big brother, I've always looked up to you and thought you loved me. Of course, just because I believed that doesn't mean you wouldn't hurt me.

I guess, where love is involved, there's always going to be some hurt. If we didn't care, it wouldn't matter what the other person said. The day you told me I was just your little sister and didn't have any right to state my opinion about your drinking hurt. Yes, it was your business, but it was my business too. Both you and Samantha drank too much, which hurt Amy. Someone needed to speak up for her, and I did.

You were right, in a way. I have no right to tell you how to run your own life. Then you went on to tell me what a pain it was to raise me, since Mom and Dad were never around to do it. That hurt the most. I felt in the way. So, I quit visiting you, Samantha and Amy. I know you were drunk when you said it, but did it make it any less true? Was being drunk the only way I'd hear the truth from you?

In hindsight, avoiding visiting you afterward was a major mistake, as I missed time with Amy. And time with you when you got sober. Of course, Samantha never managed to kick the habit, and that was sad.

I always thought of you, Alex, and myself as a unit. A group helping each other through the dysfunction of living, or not living, with traveling parents. When they dumped us on various relatives and friends and went around the world on their travels, I thought at least we had each other. If they split us up, I think I would have fallen apart.

Maybe I depended on you too much, but I needed someone, and Alex wasn't much older than me.

I'm angry and hurt and lonely. I miss my time with my older brother: you. Maybe if I get this all out on paper, it will help me find the courage to visit you like you now want. It took hours to talk myself into going to Amy and Samantha's funeral. Even the brief wave from you that day was a relief and gave me hope. You smiled. Of course, it was a sad day, so a sad smile, but at least it was a smile.

You said you're staying sober. I don't think I can visit you if you're not. I heard you were dating Hannah. I've heard about her at the hospital. I haven't met her yet. We don't have anything to do with each other at the hospital. I don't think I could go up to her and ask about you.

I know I should gather my courage and have a few more phone calls or get together with you to find out what's going on in your life. I'm sure it's been difficult for you since their deaths. Will you insult me again? I don't think I could handle that.

Sincerely (with love),
Ashley

Ashley didn't reread the letter after she wrote it but stuck it in her school folder. She'd read it later. Her hands shook, and her mouth felt dry. She went to the kitchen and grabbed a glass of water, dropping a few ice cubes into it before taking a deep drink.

This class was going to be emotional. Maybe she shouldn't have signed up for it. She decided not to second-guess her decision any longer. She'd signed up. She was going to finish. Enough with the indecision.

She had two more letters to write. The one from Paul's point of view would probably be shorter. She'd have to write about his perspective, which might make her angrier, but she might feel less vulnerable than the first letter she'd written.

She refilled her water glass and went back to the couch. Pulling out her class notebook, she opened it to a clean page and picked up her pen from the coffee table. She leaned back against the couch and started writing.

Dear Ashley,

She paused and wondered, what would Paul say? She hadn't talked to him since he became sober, except for his brief phone call when he apologized. She'd have to guess for this letter. Maybe the point of the exercise was not knowing what other people thought and assuming their feelings and motives without proof.

I got tired of taking care of you and Alex without Mom and Dad's help. I always felt inadequate. It wasn't that I didn't love you. I really did. I still do. I was overwhelmed. Overwhelmed with a drinking wife and a child who wasn't getting what she needed from me or her mom.

When we fought, I guess it boiled over and spilled out. I didn't mean the awful things I said. Sometimes I remember our argument. I want to take it back, but I can't. That's the thing about saying what you're thinking at the time. It's out there, never to be returned, and people get hurt. People whom we love get hurt.

I've missed seeing you and talking to you. I've missed seeing you and Amy chatting away, aunt to niece.

We had an unusual upbringing. You seemed to be doing the best of the three of us with Mom and

Dad gone. At least that's how it looked. Alex struggled. Maybe he told me more because we were closer in age. I felt totally unable to get you through your teen years, but I tried. You were at Grandma's for those five years. It was a long time without you. That's when a mom or dad is needed. I faltered and started drinking. I guess that's when I left the two of you alone too much.

  I hope we can get together and be a family again.

Love,
Paul

  The letter from Paul's point of view was harder to write. She stuck the letter in her folder with the other one. Deciding she was done with that part of the assignment for now, she grabbed her glass of water from the coffee table and took a drink.

  The next part of the assignment was to find a reference from the textbook pertaining to her situation with her sibling. She needed to find a reference about fighting siblings or reconciliation, or something similar. She'd enjoy her water and then look it up to see what it said.

  Dr. Athena ran her class in an unusual way. It was certainly different than her other instructors. It would be interesting to see how it would play out when everyone was reading a different part of the textbook.

CHAPTER 10

By the time Jason talked to his dad that Friday, the clinic was already closed. An on-call doctor could help, but Madison wanted her own doctor to write the prescription. That meant waiting until Tuesday morning because of Labor Day on Monday.

They'd have to wait three more days to get medication for her. Hopefully, she continued to agree she needed the medication by the time Tuesday arrived. She could change her mind one hundred times in the next few days. Who knew what would happen on Tuesday?

He decided to try and convince Madison her doctor would have noted in her chart exactly what medication she would prescribe. The only thing the on-call staff needed to do was look at the chart and prescribe whatever her regular doctor suggested. That might be the best thing to do.

He wanted to talk to his parents without Madison overhearing them. They needed to discuss who would be most likely to convince her not to wait until Tuesday. There was a better way to get through the days until her depression lifted.

After breakfast, his chance came. Madison took Chloe into her bedroom to change her diaper, and Jason suggested to his mother they take a walk in the beautiful fall day. The leaves were starting to change color, and the morning temperature was especially comfortable.

He peeked into Madison's room. "Mom and I are taking a walk. Chloe will like the falling leaves, so I'll take her along. Are you okay with that?"

"Sure," Madison said.

He picked Chloe up from the crib and told Madison she should yell out the door if she needed something. "We'll be back soon."

When he and his mom were outside, he said, "We need to talk about Madison. Let's go find Dad and have a conversation."

Patricia glanced sideways at him. "What happened yesterday while we were gone?"

"Madison had a major meltdown. I came home to find her crying on the outside step and Chloe crying in her crib. I settled Chloe down, and then Madison. I told her to take a nap, and I left Chloe with Nina while I did chores. Later I went back and picked up Chloe again.

"I talked to Madison, and she agreed to take medication but wants to wait for her own doctor to prescribe them. She won't be back in the office until Tuesday. The on-call staff can prescribe the medicine based on her chart, but Madison says she wants to wait," Jason said.

They found his dad working on a seeding machine, getting it ready for the next spring planting.

"I told Mom about Madison agreeing to take the medication but wanting to wait until her own doctor is back in the office. I don't think we should wait," Jason said.

His dad frowned at him. "What are we supposed to do? She can be stubborn. I'm not sure we should push her now she's agreed. What do you think?" He lifted his ball cap up and scratched at his balding head before putting it back on.

His mother put her hand on his arm. "We can't wait. I agree with Jason. After yesterday, we can't leave her alone with Chloe either. She could fall apart again anytime. How are we going to manage? We could take Nina into our confidence. She can help with Chloe, but we need to get Madison well. It's going to take a while even on the medication."

His dad looked at her. "Maybe you should tell her your story."

His mom shook her head before he finished his sentence. "She doesn't need to know."

"Why not? It would help her feel like she isn't alone. She probably believes no one understands. And why does it matter to you now? It's nothing to be ashamed about, is it?"

Jason had no idea what his parents were discussing.

"No." She didn't sound convinced.

"Just think about it." His dad took her hand and held it, then pulled her closer and hugged her.

Jason rarely saw physical displays from his parents. That hug, and the secret she wanted to keep, reminded him his parents had pasts he knew nothing about. "Who should talk to her?" He was sorry to break up the moment, but Madison would start wondering what was going on soon.

"I'll talk to her," his mother said. She slipped out of her husband's embrace. Then she leaned forward and kissed him. "You're right. She needs to know. Why don't you stay out here and tell Jason? I'll go talk to Madison."

His dad smiled gently at her and nodded. Jason watched his mother walk slowly back to the house. When she left them, he turned to his dad.

"Let's get to work on this seeder," his dad said.

"What do you want me to do?"

"Hold that end steady while I work on this end." He grabbed a wrench and started twisting while Jason held the end of the steel steady. He should have brought a pair of gloves outside with him to help keep a grip. He held Chloe and only had one hand free. He could feel the steel digging into his hands.

Jason tapped his hand on the steel, and his dad stopped what he was doing. "I need to get gloves, Dad. If we're going to work on this, I'll need to take Chloe back to the house. I don't want to interrupt Mom and Madison." He let go of his end. Chloe was looking around, contented to be held in his arms.

"I don't need help. I was trying to decide how to tell you." He took a deep breath and let it out. "Your mom had postpartum depression after Madison was born. She had a tough time, and she didn't want to take medication either. She never did.

"We made it through, but I wish she'd taken the medication. It's a disease that hasn't been understood for years. While she was lucky enough to have a good doctor, it was difficult being isolated on the farm, in addition to being depressed. They've come a long way in treatment and understanding, but there are people who consider you're weak if you get treatment. Believe me, there's nothing weak about your mother."

Jason walked over and patted his dad on the shoulder. It was the most serious thing his dad had said in a long time. When Jason was younger, he got a few lectures on cars and girls and respecting other people, but this was more personal. "Thanks for telling me, Dad. I certainly won't spread it around. That's up to Mom. I'm sure it will help Madison to know Mom understands what's happening to her."

"To a certain extent, it'll help. Madison has to live with those dark feelings, and that's hard. I hope she tries the medication. We'll have to see what happens and be there for her."

His dad took off his ball cap and wiped the sweat off his forehead. Then he put the cap back on his head and picked up the wrench.

"You know I'll do anything I can." He hugged his dad, and his dad hugged him back. "Thanks for telling me. Since you don't need my help, I'm going to take Chloe for a walk while Mom and Madison talk. I'll be back in a while."

His dad nodded and then started tapping with the wrench.

Jason got the feeling his dad wasn't doing anything. He walked in the direction of the creek. He always went there to think. He wanted to call Ashley and talk to her. Something about the sibling class she was taking—or anything. How had she done with her sibling relationship letters? Maybe it would help him sort it out if he put his own feelings about Madison on paper.

He wandered around the farm for a good half hour, enjoying the nice temperature and the free time. He rarely spent time wandering these days. There was always work to be done.

The leaves were starting to look golden on the maple trees. Chloe giggled at the falling leaves and jerked in his arms when one of them hit her on the nose, but then she smiled again at the fluttering colorful leaves.

The stream near their wheatfield trickled softly. He could cross it this time of year because the water was shallow in most spots. He knew where he could cross, but he didn't want to chance slipping with Chloe in his arms. He stood there, watching the water slowly meander along.

He took his phone out of his pocket to check for messages. None. His friends ignored him over the summer when he was busy on the farm. He should get in touch with them again. Maybe going out with them would take his mind off Ashley for a while.

Brad would be a good person to call. He helped his dad on their farm too, and he was probably ready for company. Maybe they could go out for the evening. Hopefully his parents would be able to watch over Madison and Chloe.

Even if Madison decided to take medication, they'd been told it would take at least three weeks to see any changes and know if it helped at all. Then there would be possible adjustments in dosage. He thought about his mom suffering from the same depression. She probably didn't want Madison to feel bad because it didn't sound like his mom had

postpartum depression after his birth. She'd kept her
secret all these years.

CHAPTER 11

Ashley was deep into reading fiction books for fun. She rarely had the chance in the past few years, as she was usually studying or working. She found after writing the first draft of the letters to Paul and from Paul, she needed to get out of her own head.

She chose a cozy mystery she checked out from the library online. She knew if she'd gone to the library to check out a book, she'd wander around the shelves and bring home more books than she'd have time to read. Her mind wandered too much during the first few chapters. She worried about her relationship with her brothers and wondered what Jason was doing today.

She finally got immersed in the story and was deep into guessing the guilty party of the murder. Her phone rang, and she almost ignored it. She was so wrapped up in the book. One look at the call log changed her mind.

"Hi, Jason," she said as she scrambled to hold the phone and set her tablet down beside her on the couch.

"Hi. What are you up to?" His voice sounded different from his usual calm tones.

"Reading a book. What's going on with you? You sound upset," Ashley said.

"I am upset. Madison won't take meds until Tuesday, and she's a mess. I don't know how we got to this point."

"Since you called and told me this, I'm assuming you're open to talking about what's going on with her."

"Well, I needed someone to talk to, and since you've taken those psychology courses, I thought I'd talk to you," he said.

She felt her heart stutter. He called because she knew a little psychology? She wasn't very knowledgeable in the situation with his sister. He was one of the few guys she had gone out with in a long time, and it had only been coffee and lunch. She believed he liked her.

"I'm sorry. That didn't come out right. I meant I really wanted to talk to you, and I'm using the fact you might know more than me to call you. I would talk to you anyway. Do you still want to talk to me after my failed attempt at conversation?"

He sounded like he meant he would call her even if she couldn't help him. "You know I can't give out advice. I'm just an undergrad, and I haven't even met your sister," Ashley said.

"How about this: I'm a guy calling to talk to my friend about my sister? Does that work? Because that's what this is. There's nothing you can do anyway. She has her own therapist, and her own pigheadedness." The frustration in his voice rang through clearly.

"Yes. We can talk as friends." She relaxed a little. He really wanted to talk to her as a friend, not because of her psychology background.

"I came home to find my sister sitting on the front step of the house having a major meltdown. It's postpartum depression. She refused medication in the past. I thought she changed her mind and planned to try them. Then Mom talked to her and shared her own experience. She didn't take medications because of the stigma back then. She hid her illness. My sister said if Mom got by without them, she didn't need them either. I wanted her to at least try them."

"No luck, hmm. Your Mom meant well," Ashley said.

"She tried to get Madison to take the medication and not wait. Mom said if she had to do it over again, she would have tried. I don't know why my sister is so opposed to them; except she said it would make her feel weak to take them. To top it off, she starts her senior year Tuesday after Labor Day, which means more pressure for her with homework and getting to school every day," Jason said. "Mom cried after her talk with Madison because her story changed my sister's mind again on the medication."

"I have a feeling your sister will change her mind again pretty quickly. She'll probably only make it to school for a few days, and then find it too strenuous for her. You might need to suggest she take classes at home. I would hope the school would be open to that plan. She can get rest throughout the day," Ashley tried to reassure him.

"I hoped her going to school would be a good thing. She sleeps a lot already because of her depression. However, it's hard to know how much sleep she's getting because she sleeps at odd times and is awake in the middle of the night." Jason sounded desperate.

Ashley wondered if she dare broach the subject but decided it couldn't hurt. "Do you pray, Jason?" She didn't wait for him to answer. "Maybe this is a time to ask God for help. Ask Him to help you do the best thing for your sister."

Silence descended on the other end of the phone, and she waited. There was no way to know his feelings until he voiced something one way or another. He hadn't hung up on her, anyway.

"You've got a good idea," he finally said. "I do go to church, but I have to say, my daily prayer life isn't consistent."

Ashley's shoulders relaxed. He didn't sound mad. "Mine either. I even avoid church. I guess I'm mad at God for giving me the family I have, so I stay away. The class I'm taking about siblings is harder than I anticipated. We're not exactly reconciled at the moment."

"Writing these letters for class is bringing up bad feelings?" Jason asked.

"It's bringing those feelings to the front of my mind. I've been busy trying to get my psychology degree, so I've been able to avoid thinking about the situation for years. I considered quitting the class. Then I decided to stick it out. I guess I want my brothers back in my life. Dr. Athena might have the answers I need." She hoped. Her parents were off jetting around the world, and she'd probably never have a real relationship with them. Her brothers were another story. They had been close once. They could be again.

"I haven't even started my homework on the speech we need to write. I've been too busy dealing with Madison's issues." His laugh was bitter. "I'm sorry. I'm sounding whiny. I'm tired, and we don't have a solution for my sister. Until we find one, this situation is going to continue. At least harvest is over, and there's not as much to do around the farm," Jason said.

"You're going to have homework. Madison is going to have homework and spells of depression, so you feel overwhelmed," Ashley said sympathetically.

"Exactly. You know, you're going to make a great therapist if you continue on with classes. If you don't, you'll always be a great friend to talk to. Thanks for listening. I'm done with my moping."

"You're welcome to call any time you need someone to listen." She was getting more comfortable with the idea of a friendship with Jason. Jill would be happy about her taking more chances in her relationships.

She and Jason were certainly starting out with some complex situations. His sister's depression, and Ashley's family dysfunction. That was life.

What did God want her to do? Probably help Jason when possible. Besides, that wasn't difficult since she liked him.

"I'll be taking you up on the calls. Mainly because I like talking to you," Jason said.

Ashley felt warmth flood her face and was glad he couldn't see her blush. "Thank you."

"I'm looking forward to our next coffee lunch date," he said.

She cleared her throat. "Me too."

"Talk to you soon."

She could hardly say goodbye through the lump in her throat. Nerves jangled as she hung up the phone. She was not good with relationships. Hiding herself away for years hadn't been healthy. Plus, it made the learning curve steep, but Jason was worth it.

CHAPTER 12

The weekend passed quickly for Ashley. After spending Saturday cleaning and reading, she slept soundly. Sunday, she and Jill attended the ten a.m. church service and went out for brunch. Then Jill worked the evening shift.

Ashley took her two letters out of the homework folder and reworded them as much as she could. She read the assigned book passages.

Labor Day came too soon. She spent her last free day before going back to work taking photographs of the autumn leaves and other pretty views around the city. She enjoyed landscape photos. When she was younger, she liked taking pictures of people and their facial expressions. Now she preferred taking pictures of scenery.

The brilliant blue sky shone, and the birds chirped insistently. She spent a lot of time thinking about Jason and Paul. She couldn't continue to let her abandonment issues run her life.

So, her parents left her with other people and signed their parental rights over to her grandmother when she was a teenager. One of her brothers had a snit when he was drunk. The other brother and his wife tried to save her reputation by keeping her out of their lives once he went to jail. When she summed it up, she realized that all of it had shaped her. Yes, it was hard, but it wasn't the worst thing to happen.

She needed to decide if she was going to continue with school or start job hunting. She hadn't signed up for any classes or even applied to the master's in psychology program. That should have told her something right there. She wasn't committed to the plan she had when she started school. She groaned. She had no plans at all.

She did know she wanted to be closer to her brothers. Since one lived in Bismarck, and one lived in Chokecherry Valley, her best option would be to stay in North Dakota. If she decided to work, the job market would probably be best in Bismarck unless she moved west to Dickinson.

To start on her plan to get closer to her brothers again, the first step would be to see Courtney. With Alex getting out of prison in December, Courtney would need all the friends she could get. If she planned to patch up her differences with her brothers, she might as well visit her sister-in-law.

#

Ashley hadn't seen Courtney for two years. When Alex went to prison for embezzlement, Ashley's visit with Courtney hadn't gone well. Courtney told her she didn't need sympathy or pity. She had no idea how Courtney would react when Ashley arrived at their house in Chokecherry Valley. When she'd called to tell her she was coming to visit, there had been no answer. She'd tried visiting when Alex first went to prison, but

Courtney refused to come to the door. This time, Ashley wasn't taking no for an answer.

On the hour drive out to Chokecherry Valley that afternoon, Ashley considered Alex's situation. She'd wanted to go visit her brother in prison, but Alex didn't want any visitors. Ashley didn't understand why not. She had even gone to the prison, only to have Alex refuse to see her.

She hadn't been judgmental when he was on trial. All the proof against him seemed to be solid, and Alex hadn't fought at all. Ashley didn't understand that either. Alex hadn't put up much of a defense. When he could have hired a better lawyer, he didn't. She volunteered to help pay, and both Alex and Courtney adamantly told her to stay out of it. They knew what they were doing.

The whole situation confused her. Alex and Courtney weren't big spenders, and Ashley's parents gave all their children plenty of money to live on and go to school. Alex's job at the bank paid well. She suspected they kept important parts of the situation between the two of them.

The turnoff from the highway to Chokecherry Valley came closer, and her hands got sweaty on the steering wheel. She breathed faster. She prayed for calm and peace.

The worst that could happen had already happened. Courtney and Alex turned her away two years ago. Courtney might do the same again today, but Ashley was two years older and more mature now than she'd been on her last visit. She'd insist on a good reason from Courtney not to stay in touch.

Courtney had a big family, and Ashley knew she hadn't cut them off. She hadn't seen Courtney for so long, maybe she hid from her own family too. It was time for the truth.

Ashley planned to contact Paul anyway, and if Courtney turned her away again, she would bring Paul with her next time. One thing she knew: she wouldn't give up easily this time. She missed her brothers and Courtney. With Samantha's and Amy's deaths, she realized how short life could be.

Courtney and Alex lived at the end of Main Street on five acres of land, so they were slightly set apart from the town. The house had been owned by Ashley's parents. When they gave money to all their children, Alex wanted the house. Ashley and Paul were intent on getting out of Chokecherry Valley and going to college.

Ashley had always wanted to major in psychology. She wasn't sure Paul had always wanted to be a doctor. Alex had been content to get his four-year bachelor's degree in business and was fortunate that he happened to graduate just when the previous bank manager retired.

Alex and Courtney met in college and got married right after graduation. Alex worked at the bank for three years before the charge of embezzlement derailed their life. Ashley couldn't believe it when she heard about it. The amount of money was small, and Alex didn't need it.

Their parents settled a lot of money on each of them before they went off to travel around the world. She always thought of it as guilty conscience money. She needed it to live, so she hadn't turned the gift down. She dreamed of paying them back in full and totally divorcing herself from her parents. The whole situation irritated her.

She pulled up in front of Alex and Courtney's house. She expected Courtney to be home because it was a holiday, but she no longer knew if Courtney worked or not. If she changed her job to retail, or something similar, she might not have the day off. With Alex's reputation in shreds, Courtney's life must have imploded. Ashley didn't know what happened, and it made her mad.

She got out of the vehicle and approached the front door. The white house looked well-kept on the outside. A wrap-around veranda with a porch swing on each side of the front door sported colorful red and navy pillows and cushions. The curtains were open in the front window and the kitchen.

She knew from growing up in the house, the kitchen was on the left, and the living room on the right when you entered. Alex did minimal remodeling. He removed the wall between the kitchen and the living room to make it all one space. Otherwise, he left the structure alone.

Ashley walked up the stairs to the front door and knocked. While she waited, she looked back down Main Street. The grocery store and a small café were open for business. There weren't many other businesses along the street. Most people went to a few of the bigger towns in the area for anything else, such as medical care or more shopping variety. The bar, bank, and a gas station were the only other businesses. The bank and bar looked closed now, probably because of Labor Day.

She waited another five minutes and then sat on one of the porch swings, gently swinging. It felt good to be back in Chokecherry Valley. It had been great to move out of town to go to school, but time had passed. She felt nostalgic for the times she had lived in the house with Paul and Alex during weekends when her grandmother needed a break.

Obviously, Courtney wasn't home. Ashley had peeked into the garage, which was empty, and no vehicles were parked in front of the house. Ashley looked down Main Street again. Should she ask at one of the open businesses? Courtney might even be working at one of them. Or maybe she went to her parents' house in Bismarck for the long weekend.

She had decided to go back to her vehicle when she heard a car headed her way from the back of the house, not from Main Street.

The woman parked in the driveway. At first, Ashley didn't recognize the driver. From this distance, she noticed short, choppy purple hair, and the glint of the sun caught something glittery.

Ashley watched her sit in her vehicle for a minute. She realized it was Courtney, and she didn't hurry to get out of the car to talk to her. She hadn't shut off the engine either. Ashley hoped she wouldn't leave.

Finally, the engine died, and Courtney leaned over to the passenger seat. She straightened up again and opened the driver's door. She struggled to get out with her purse while juggling a pile of books in her hands.

Ashley stood up from the swing. "Would you like help with those books?"

Courtney stared at her for a moment before answering, "Sure."

Ashley moved forward and took some of them from her, and Courtney managed the rest. Looking at the top title, she realized they were library books. She didn't know Courtney liked to read. She looked up. "I wasn't sure I'd get to see you today. I'm glad I waited."

"I told you I didn't want to see you." Courtney walked to the front door, rummaged in her purse, and eventually pulled out a key. She stuck it in the lock and turned it, then opened the door. She turned to Ashley, reaching out for the books. "Thank you."

Ashley hung on to the books. "I'll bring them inside."

"Not necessary. You can set them on the porch swing," she said in a dull monotone.

Ashley didn't like the lack of life in her voice. "No. I'm coming in. I imagine you can call someone to chase me off, but I plan to talk to you today. I drove an hour here, and I'll be driving an hour home. I waited on your porch. I'm not leaving until we've discussed this situation.

"Alex is getting out of jail soon, and I plan to visit him. I shouldn't have listened to you before when you told me not to visit, but I was too young to know better. Well, I know better now. Life is short, and I'm not leaving until we discuss this." She took a deep breath and then let it out. The long speech had been brewing ever since her decision to visit.

Courtney must have realized the futility of arguing. She didn't say anything, but when she went into the house, she left the door open. Ashley took it as an invitation to enter, which she did quickly before Courtney changed her mind.

From the entryway, Ashley looked around curiously at her childhood home. Alex and Courtney hadn't changed much since they purchased the home from Paul and Ashley. The floor plan was still an open living room, dining room, and kitchen.

They took out the carpet and replaced it with wood floors. The walls were all painted a soft creamy white instead of the light blue color her mother favored at one time. Her mother had gotten into a country vibe and hung gingham curtains in the kitchen. Ashley changed them in her senior year to a lacy cream panel over a cream blind. Courtney and Alex must have liked them because they were still there.

She realized while she'd been taking stock of the room, her sister-in-law was watching her. "You want to sit down and get comfortable?" Courtney asked, settling herself on the plush blue couch where she dumped the books and her purse.

Ashley added the books she'd been carrying onto the pile on the couch and took a seat on the matching chair across from Courtney. Now she'd cornered her, she didn't know quite how to build the bridge back to some sort of relationship. "How are you doing?"

"Well, people talk to me when they walk into the grocery store now. They used to totally ignore me."

"Why didn't you move? You know I would have helped you, and so would Paul."

Courtney's expression hardened. "You would have, but Paul..." She shrugged.

Ashley nodded. "Yes, I suppose it wouldn't have worked." She decided to keep her own feelings about how Paul treated her to herself. "I would have shared an apartment with you and helped you find a job."

"I know." Her face softened. "Listen, Ashley. I get what you want. I have a big family. I know how it works. There are things about the situation Alex and I didn't share with anyone. We made the decision together to keep you from being in the middle of it. You were going to school and had a dream to be a psychologist. Alex and I didn't want to ruin your life too."

Ashley's heart pounded uncomfortably fast. "I wanted to talk to him."

"He didn't let you visit him in prison, did he?"

"No. He refused to see me."

"He did it to protect you."

Ashley felt tears welling. Finding out Courtney and Alex discussed how to exclude her from their lives hurt, even if they believed it was for her own good. "I wish you two would have included me in that discussion."

"I'm pretty sure we knew what you would say."

Ashley blinked, and then sniffed.

Courtney got her a tissue from the kitchen. "I'm sorry we hurt you, but you don't know what it's been like around here in Chokecherry Valley since they convicted Alex."

Ashley wiped her nose and, taking a deep breath, sat up straight. "I could have handled it."

Courtney shook her head. "It's difficult. Plus, that's not the point. Alex didn't want you to have to handle it. He and I made the decision for him to plead guilty. He didn't want you to suffer for his actions. He was glad you were away at school and wouldn't be in Chokecherry Valley. The farther away you were, the better he assumed it would be for you."

"What about you? You were left alone to manage it," Ashley said.

"I wasn't. You know I have a big family. They came and hung around with me until the talk died down to a dull roar, and I was an occasional footnote in the gossip."

Ashley felt a pang of longing when Courtney said her family helped her through the last few years. Paul and Alex basically deserted her, and she'd been on her own. It was the reason she couldn't readily open herself up to a relationship. At her age, she felt she should have had at least a boyfriend or two, but she didn't trust them not to leave her. Meeting Jason opened her eyes to missed possibilities.

Her parents left her and her brothers to the kindness of others. They'd never been warm and loving. Ashley longed for a family, but not like her family. She wanted a close one like Courtney's family.

It amazed her she could envy her sister-in-law, who dealt with Alex's actions at the bank and the poor reputation he'd created. It couldn't have been easy to stay in the town and work.

"I have my job. It's only me and the owner. She's kind to me and frowns at anyone making rude comments. They pretty much leave me alone. It's okay, Ashley. Alex will be home soon," Courtney said.

Ashley thought Courtney's voice held a hint of tears, but she had built a shell around herself, so it was hard to tell. She stood up. "I'm going to go now. You seem to have everything you need. I want you to know, I would have been here for you. I'm available for you now."

Courtney stood too, and they looked at each other across the coffee table. "I know. But Alex—"

Ashley interrupted with a smile. "He said no. Got it. I'm a few years older now, and this time I'm not listening." She walked to the door. "I'll be back to see you soon."

She walked down the steps and over to her car, smiling to herself. She made progress in patching up part of the relationship between herself and Courtney. They'd at least had a conversation in the house instead of on the front step.

CHAPTER 13

Jason emerged from the grocery store and saw Ashley come out of the Richmonds' house. He hadn't realized she knew anyone in Chokecherry Valley when they'd first met. Now he knew Paul and Alex were her brothers, he figured she was visiting Courtney. He knew Alex was still in prison. As soon as he got out, the news would be all over town.

If she'd been a child in Chokecherry Valley, how had he never known her before he saw her in class? This was a small town. He must have met her when they were young, and it hadn't registered. Her explanation of being with her grandmother in Bismarck during high school explained why he didn't know her from those years.

He ducked back into the grocery store. As much as he wanted to talk to her, he needed to get back to the farm.

"Is there something you need, Jason?" Betty asked.

He looked back at the owner, who ran the store today. "No. I'm fine." His face flushed. He glanced out the glass window, watching as Ashley backed out of the driveway. He looked at Betty again. "I have a feeling I forgot something. Thought if I stepped back inside, I might remember."

"Anything coming to you?" Betty glanced out the window too. Without waiting for him to answer, she asked, "Do you know the woman coming out of Courtney's house? She looks familiar to me."

He shook his head, then changed his mind. "Ashley Richmond. She's in one of my college classes."

"Oh. That's Ashley? Alex's sister. I suppose she came to talk to Courtney since Alex is getting out of jail soon."

Jason nodded. He didn't want to discuss Ashley. He needed to get back to watch Chloe and Madison so his mom could do what she needed to do. He had lots of homework because last night he spent too much of his time thinking about Ashley.

At least Betty wasn't a gossip. She didn't push any further conversation on him.

"Well, if I've forgotten something, I can't remember what it is." He smiled at Betty, and she smiled back.

"I'll see you soon." He walked back outside to his vehicle, wondering if Betty was watching him leave. It didn't matter. He couldn't feel any more foolish than he already did.

The puzzle of Ashley and why he didn't recognize her from Chokecherry Valley would remain a mystery. He had other things to take care of this weekend.

Madison seemed to be doing better since the family banded together to make sure she got her rest and got breaks from taking care of Chloe. Jason didn't mind the extra work if Madison improved.

His trepidation centered around what would happen once school started on Tuesday. It was Madison's senior year, and she decided to go to school instead of trying to get her G.E.D. online. He hoped her getting out of the house and seeing other people throughout the day would help her mood. It concerned him that having to get up every day and get to school, do homework, and take care of Chloe all together might prove too much for her. She might get more depressed.

He'd talked to their mom about it, and she'd advised waiting for the end of the first week of school to see what happened. At least the school week only lasted four days because of Labor Day.

He hoped it wouldn't matter. Maybe he worried for nothing, but he felt Madison would crash with one more thing added to her plate. Maybe he should be more positive about the situation. Time would tell.

When he opened the front door of their farmhouse, the smell of freshly baked cookies greeted him. He looked at the counter. Chocolate peanut butter. His favorite.

His mom came into the room carrying her purse. "Nina and I are going over to the Millers to see if they need anything before winter comes. We want to make sure they're doing okay in their new home."

"We did hurry to put things together when they had that fire. Let me know if you and Nina need help with anything. I'm sure Dad and I can do any repairs or find someone who can."

His mom settled her purse in the crook of her arm and leaned over to pat his hand, which rested on the counter near the cookies. "I know, dear. You're always so kind. What did your dad and

I do to deserve such great kids and a wonderful grandchild?"

"I don't know—and I'm not sure what I did to deserve chocolate peanut butter cookies either."

The glint in his mother's eyes should have warned him. "They're not for you."

He frowned at her as she headed toward the door to leave. With her hand on the knob, she turned and smiled at him. "Just kidding. Help yourself."

He smiled back, and then turned to scoop up a few cookies. He heard her laughter as she closed the door behind her. His mother had a great sense of humor. It had been a long time since he'd heard her laughing, he realized, which meant she was worried. Worried and stressed.

Something needed to change. If Madison couldn't handle school, he'd talk her into online schooling and medication. At least she could try it. He should probably research the medication angle. Maybe it wouldn't be good for Madison.

Ashley might know. Other than calling her, when would he have time to get together with her? As much as he wanted to date her, now wasn't a good time. She would continue with more classes or look for a job. Maybe even move away, depending on what she decided she wanted for her future.

He was trying to take a full load of classes, work on the farm, and take care of Madison and Chloe. His mother was already stressed out and worried. As much as he liked Ashley, he shouldn't add one more thing to his life. As much as he argued with himself, he knew what he was going to

do: spend as much time with Ashley as possible.
They'd work it out.

CHAPTER 14

Ashley arrived at class early on Wednesday. She hoped Jason would be there, and she could talk to him. He walked into class with Dr. Williams, so she had no chance to ask him how his long weekend had gone or how Madison made it through. She'd spent way too much time over the weekend thinking about him and hoping they could get together after class again today.

He smiled and said hello to her as he sat down, and then Dr. Williams started the class. He went over some extra information about different types of speeches and mentioned there was a sign-up sheet for the students to choose a date to give their speeches.

"We have time for three speeches per class, so we can discuss the presentation after each speech."

She planned to write her first speech as quickly as possible and practice once in front of Jason. Then she would sign up for the first opening that would reasonably give her time to be ready. Hopefully, she would have a few minutes to talk to Jason about when he would be available to practice their speeches. If not, she could text him and ask.

She sent a sideways look at him, but he was concentrating on Dr. Williams. She started listening too, and it helped take her mind off her own churning thoughts.

When class ended, Jason quickly got his stuff together and said a quick goodbye. "Busy day with Chloe since Madison is in school," he explained. "I'll call you when I get a minute."

She gathered her own things as he walked out the classroom door. Well. She'd worried all weekend about being nervous at lunch with him today, and he didn't have time.

She told herself not to be hurt. It wasn't his fault he needed to watch Chloe, but Ashley was disappointed. She had wanted to have lunch with him, even if it made her nervous.

She had enough to keep herself busy for the day. She got home, ate quickly, and went to work. Being at work reminded her she needed to set up a meeting with Paul.

She wondered if she'd seen Paul's girlfriend at work yet. Since she didn't know what the woman looked like, it was hard to know. She was kind of surprised she hadn't run into Paul in the hallway either, but they were in different parts of the large building. She'd only been at work for a few afternoons too. Different hallways, stairways, and elevators to use. He probably stayed in his department seeing patients and eating lunch in his office or their staff lounge.

She wanted to see him from a distance first. Maybe she should go over to his side of the building and skulk around. She laughed at the idea. That was ridiculous. The best thing to do would be call him and set up a time to meet. Getting together with him as soon as possible would calm the butterflies flipping around in her stomach. She hoped.

Telling him how hurt she felt by how he treated her two years ago and setting some parameters for future times she saw him would go a long way toward showing her where she stood with him. If they were going to get closer, she needed to follow through and get courageous.

CHAPTER 15

Ashley called Paul on her break at work. Their conversation was stilted but cordial. They set up a time to meet for dinner that evening. She hadn't expected him to be free right away, but his eagerness to see her was a good sign. She wanted to get together with him but assumed she'd have a little more time to get used to the idea. It was better she didn't have time to ruminate.

She chose a quiet bistro she loved. It would be a good place to talk.

She saw Jill for a few minutes between work and going out to meet Paul. Work had kept her busy, but now her stomach cramped at the idea of seeing him.

Jill looked her over when she came out of the bedroom. "You look nice in your pink blouse and jeans, but you're pale. Are you okay?"

"I'm fine. Just nervous about seeing Paul, you know?" She gripped her purse in one hand and rubbed her head with the other.

"He's your brother, and he wants to mend your relationship. He'll be on his best behavior," Jill tried to reassure her.

"You're right. I need to remember him from when we were younger and not when he drank. He lost his wife and daughter. I imagine that has made him more sympathetic. I don't want to get hurt again if he suddenly changes."

"You don't have to give your whole heart over to him today, silly." Jill slung her leg over the couch arm and lay back on the couch.

Ashley envied her. She wanted to forget meeting Paul and join Jill for a relaxing night of movies and popcorn.

"Hey, look at it this way: it'll take your mind off what's-his-name from your class." Jill grinned at her.

"Funny. You know what his name is." Jill did have a point. If she kept busy talking to Paul, she wouldn't wonder if Jason would have time for lunch after their next class. She knew he was busy with his sister and other things. She had to be patient and give him the space he needed to take care of his responsibilities.

#

She arrived at the bistro before Paul and sat at a table along one of the walls. She liked it there better than one of the tables in the middle of the room. The waiter arranged two menus and asked for her drink order.

"I'll have water for now. Thank you."

He left, and Paul arrived soon after, his face lit up with a smile. "Hi, there," he said as he took his seat.

She smiled back. She wasn't ready to hug him yet. "Hi. It's good to see you."

He looked much better than at the funeral. He appeared less weary and less uptight than she'd seen him in years. Even when he drank, he had a stressed look around his mouth and eyes. Like everything in life was difficult.

"Let's order first, and then talk," he suggested.

She liked the idea. Maybe her nerves would settle while he looked at the menu.

"What's good to eat here?" Paul asked.

"Pretty much everything. I've never had a bad meal. I'm having a shrimp salad."

Paul smiled again. "You always did like seafood."

She laughed. "You used to call me a fish. I never did learn how to swim."

He laughed too. "I'm going to have the chicken alfredo with broccoli."

"I've eaten it, and it's good here." The small talk and his easy manner calmed her down, she realized. Whatever happened after Samantha's and Amy's deaths relaxed him in a way she'd never seen before. Even when they were children moving from place to place, he'd been high-strung.

"I never told you in person. I'm sorry about Samantha and Amy."

They were interrupted by the waiter bringing the bread and olive oil dip with seasoning. When the waiter left with Paul's drink order and their meal order, Paul acknowledged her words. "Thank you. I appreciated you coming to the funeral. It meant the world to me."

He took a piece of bread but didn't dip it in the oil or take a bite. He looked at it for a minute and then set it on his plate. He looked over at her. "I'm sorry for what I said when I was drunk that day. It was inexcusable, but I hope someday you can forgive me. I know you came to the funeral and agreed to meet me this evening, but I don't know if we can ever have the sibling relationship I want. I don't know what you want, and I'm not going to put you on the spot by asking you. I appreciate any time you can spend with me."

As Ashley listened to him, he sounded sincere. He left it up to her whether she wanted to talk to him or not. She knew she wouldn't have come this evening if she didn't want to see him or talk to him again.

The waiter came by again with a tray holding their main courses, a water pitcher, and Paul's glass of water. After he placed everything on the table and refilled Ashley's water glass, he left them alone again.

Ashley used the time to plan what she wanted to say. "You'll always be my brother, Paul. That's never going to change. Yes, I was hurt when you said I was a nuisance, and you'd rather not see me again.

"Maybe I didn't have the right to talk to you about Samantha the way I did, but I couldn't ignore the fact she and you were both drinking to excess while taking care of Amy. I felt you should do something, and you brushed me off. Rudely. I was concerned about Amy." She didn't add that it had resulted in tragedy in the end. Her brother knew all too well.

The smile left his face, and she saw the deep grooves of grief in his features. He had lost weight, which enhanced those grooves. The smile hid the extent of his pain.

"You were right, and I paid the price. I'm not going to hide behind excuses. When I got sober two years ago, I should have taken further action to protect Amy. I didn't."

"I'm sorry that happened," Ashley said. "I forgive you, Paul. I really do. I've considered getting in contact with you a lot in the past year, but I didn't have the guts. I'm glad you called. I do want to spend time with you too."

His face relaxed again. "I'm glad. I've missed you. I didn't realize until I heard your voice on the phone the other day just how much." He picked up his fork to start eating.

While they both needed to let the matter settle for a while and gradually form a new relationship, she had one more thing to say. "Paul, I need to tell you, if you start drinking again, I'll do what I can to help. However, I won't put up with you treating me badly again."

"Understood," he said.

She picked up her fork and started on her salad. They ate in silence for a while. She was surprised she had an appetite, but with the initial conversation behind them, she relaxed.

When Paul took a drink of his water and cleared his throat, Ashley almost laughed. He always cleared his throat when he had something important to say. She hoped it was about something good.

He put his fork back on his plate. "I met someone at the hospital. Her name is Hannah, and she makes me happy."

"Great, Paul. I'm glad for you." She didn't tell him she'd heard rumors.

"We're dating right now, but I did buy her an engagement ring this summer. I told her about it and asked her to let me know when she was ready. She wants to wait until a year has passed since Samantha and Amy went to Heaven."

What astonished Ashley the most about Paul's words was his use of "heaven." She hadn't realized he believed in God. She wanted to talk to him about the subject, but they were already covering a lot of ground this evening.

"Congratulations." She lifted her water glass in a toast to him. "Here's to your wonderful news."

"Thanks. I can't wait until it's formal, and my ring is on her finger."

"Did you know I'm working at the hospital where you work?" Ashley asked. "I'm taking a clinical observation course to view potential job opportunities in the field."

"I heard the rumors. That was another reason I wanted to get together with you. We didn't need to have our first meeting in a long time to happen in the hospital corridor," Paul said.

"Good point." She finished her salad and pushed her plate away. "I'm also starting to have second reconsider whether I really want to become a psychologist. The problem is, I don't have another occupation in mind."

The waiter stopped by to replenish their water and ask if they wanted anything else. They both refused dessert, and he left again.

"That must be difficult. You always knew what you wanted to do." Paul's face crinkled in concern.

"I thought I did. Sometimes life changes when we least expect it." She thought of her career but also of Paul's life.

"That's for sure. I'd really like to help you if you want to discuss other careers or anything else, Ashley. Just getting together this evening has shown me that I really missed you. I'd like to start getting together on a regular basis. Are you okay with that? I want to make up for lost time," Paul said.

Again, he left the choice to her. "You don't have to let me make the decisions about getting together, Paul. I said I forgive you, and I do. There might be some lingering hurt, but eventually that will go away. Life is short. Let's become the family we never were before. Yes, you and Alex and I hung out together, but we were young. We didn't know what was going on half the time. Let's build something better than what our parents left us to muddle around in."

Paul's smile lit up his face again. "I love your idea. Of course, we have two new people involved. I have Hannah, and Alex has Courtney. Maybe you have someone else too?"

She almost mentioned Jason, but it was too soon. She'd only known him a week and hadn't talked to him since their lunch the previous week. She felt like keeping their new relationship to herself for a while yet. She smiled back at Paul. "You never know when someone will pop up in my life. Five is a good number to start with for our family for now."

She frowned. "However, convincing Courtney and Alex to join in this family effort might be difficult. Alex told me not to visit him in prison, and Courtney basically threw me out of the house when I went to visit her after Alex was first imprisoned. I went there this past weekend and told her I wasn't staying away any longer. She grudgingly let me in, and we talked for a while."

"I tried to visit Alex too, and the same thing happened to me. He said to stay away. He didn't want to contaminate me or you with his misdeeds."

Ashley twisted the napkin on her lap. "I find it difficult to believe Alex embezzled that money. He didn't need it. Mom and Dad gave him and Courtney enough to live on, and his job at the bank paid well. It always felt strange to me, but he pled guilty. Didn't you find it strange?"

"Yes. Money never seemed important to him, and the amount was low compared to the settlement we all got from Mom and Dad. I mean, if you're going to steal, do it on a grand scale."

Ashley knew Paul was the one who did things on a grand scale. He was always all in. Alex had been the cautious one.

"Maybe he did it to see if he would get caught, and that's why he kept the amount low. I don't understand the whole situation," Paul said.

Ashley had been about to take a sip of water but set her glass down. "You don't imagine he did it just as a game?"

"He does have a bit of a sense of humor, but embezzling is going a little too far and not his usual idea of a joke. He didn't realize he'd go to prison for it. I bet if we got him to tell the truth, he'd say he assumed he'd have to pay the money back, do community service, and that would be all."

"They did decide to send him to prison. What about Courtney? Wouldn't he have wanted to protect her from the scorn of all the people in Chokecherry Valley? She lived with their sneers and vandalism all this time," Ashley said.

"He probably talked it over with her once the situation got dire, and she agreed with our banishment. He wouldn't have done that to her if she hadn't felt the same way. Courtney's tough."

Ashley shook her head and kept twisting the napkin in her hands. "If we're right, Alex should have gotten a better attorney."

"Well, when he's out of prison, I can pester him until I know the truth."

"And what good would that do? Alex did it for a purpose. It's his life and Courtney's. They must have a powerful reason for their actions."

"Oh, I have no doubt."

Ashley had doubts, but she didn't mention them to Paul. There was no reason big enough for Alex to spend two years in prison without fighting a little harder for a lighter sentence. At least he could have appealed.

"Well, I'm going to visit Courtney again this weekend. I'll be there as many weekends as I can until Alex gets home in December, which is just a few months away. I know Courtney has family, but one more person on her side can't hurt," Ashley said.

"I'm going to stop by their place the day after Alex gets out of prison. They'll need his first day home to themselves, but I'm not waiting longer than a day. If Alex hadn't refused to see me when I

went to visit him at the prison, I would have gone
there on a regular basis. Now, he can't stop me."

"Me either. Do you want to pick me up, and
I'll go with you, or do you want to go alone?"

"Let's go together." Paul picked up his
water glass and lifted it in the air. "Here's to our
new closer-knit family."

She raised her glass to him too.

CHAPTER 16

Jason woke up Friday with the feeling the situation with Madison was working out the way the family hoped. They hadn't left her alone with Chloe, and both of them appeared calmer. There was less crying. Madison seemed more engaged with Chloe, without getting overwhelmed.

Madison had gone to school for three days now and hadn't said much about it when she got home. He hoped that meant everyone treated her okay.

He showered and dressed for classes. He looked forward to seeing Ashley in class. Now that Madison spent all day in school, he could stretch out class to include lunch again. He knew his mom would watch Chloe for the extra hour it would take him to get home, as it would be a few days a week. Especially if he told her why he was late.

Did he want to tell his family about Ashley? He kept changing his mind about telling them. They would work extra hard to let him have time with her, and he didn't want them to go out of their way. The situation with Madison might be okay now, but it had only been a week since they'd made the changes. She hadn't recovered from her depression, and until then, he couldn't add a further burden on his parents.

He would tell them he was meeting a friend for lunch. In a way, Ashley's small window of time for lunch worked to his benefit. He didn't have to be the one to always hurry away from her. He already decided he wanted to see her more often, and he was trying hard not to be frustrated by the other demands on his time. From the moment when she poked him in the shoulder, and he looked up to see her smiling, he wanted to get to know her.

Humming a tune as he left the bedroom, he noticed Madison's door remained closed. He looked at the watch on his wrist. She would be late to school if she didn't get up soon. He knocked on her door.

Madison didn't answer. He knocked again. "You're going to be late."

As he listened, he heard the crib creak, but he got no response from Madison. He opened the door and poked his head into the room. Madison's bed was empty.

Chloe lay in her crib, sucking her fingers, her eyes sleepy in her sweet face as she looked at him. He went to pick her up and saw her pajamas were wet. He rubbed her cheek with his finger. "I might need to get your mom or grandma to change you."

He smiled at her, and she gurgled back. He went to find Madison or his mom.

His mom sat at the kitchen table eating toast slathered with chokecherry jelly and cereal. "Good morning."

"Good morning, honey." She looked at his clothes. "All ready to leave?"

"Yes. Chloe needs a diaper change. If you don't have time, I'll do it, but I don't want to get these clothes wet. I don't have time to change again for school."

"I'll do it. Wasn't Madison there?"

"No. She must have left for school. I didn't hear her leaving. Did you?"

His mom shook her head. "That's strange. I've been in the kitchen all morning. I should have seen her. She must have left early, but I don't understand why she would do that."

She got up and rummaged around through the papers and other items on the counter. "I don't see a note."

"No note on the fridge either," Jason said. "Why would she leave so early?" He didn't like the flutter in his stomach. She wouldn't leave early enough to miss their mom. Unless she had something to hide. The thought did nothing for the state of his stomach.

"I'll go check for her car." Jason went outside and around the corner of the house where they usually parked their vehicles. They were all there. He stood there a moment, not wanting to break the news to his mother. This was not good. He tried to call Madison on her cell but didn't get an answer.

He went back into the house. "All the vehicles are here. Maybe she got a ride from a friend." He tried her phone again and walked into her bedroom. He didn't hear it ringing in the house either.

His mother finished her breakfast and stood by the sink. "We would have heard a vehicle drive up to the house. We'll need to call the school to see if she's there." She took a deep breath as if to say something more. Instead, she pursed her lips together. "My cell phone is in the bedroom. I'll be back in a minute."

"I'll go change Chloe. At least she's been content to lay in her crib this morning, but she'll need to be fed." He got Chloe changed and dressed, then picked up her blanket and a few toys and laid her on the floor in the living room. She waved her arms and smiled, satisfied with life, which was a blessing. He expected her to be crying by now. Maybe Madison fed her before she left. He'd find out soon.

He heard his mom talking on the phone but not the words. She took longer than he expected, which didn't bode well. He knew his dad had started taking his phone with him wherever he went, even if he only went to the barn. If Mom called Dad after the school, then Madison hadn't shown up at school this morning.

He finished making Chloe's bottle. He went back to the living room, picked her up, and held her in the crook of his arm as he started feeding her. She sucked greedily, so it was hard to tell if Madison fed her or not. That didn't give him any clue as to when she left the house.

His mother came from her bedroom and stood there looking at him and Chloe. He said it for her: "She didn't go to school."

"No." She plopped down on the rocker next to the couch where Jason sat. "I don't even know if she has any friends anymore. We'll have to call around. Madison will hate that."

Jason nodded.

"I called Nina. She'll watch Chloe for us while we figure out what to do. I said we'd drop her off in about a half hour."

"That'll work. I'll skip class today. It's a good thing most of my classes are online. When I'm done feeding Chloe, I'll change into other clothes, drop Chloe off at Nina's, and then go looking on a few of the paths out here where she usually walks. Maybe she twisted an ankle or something." He tried to be upbeat and not mention worst-case scenarios.

"I talked to your dad. He'll be done with chores soon and then come back to the house."

He burped Chloe, then he reassured his mom, "We'll find her."

Her expression was doubtful. The lines on her forehead and around her mouth deepened.

"Yes, we will."

He saw her shake off her lethargy. "Yes, we will," she repeated.

He got up and set Chloe in her lap. "Here. Hold your granddaughter for a few minutes while I go change." He smiled at his mom and dropped the burp cloth on top of Chloe's lap. He went to his room and shut the door. He said a few prayers to God to keep his sister safe as he changed his clothes.

Where could his sister be? Why hadn't she left a note? Why had she skipped school? What was going on in her mind? No answers came.

His mom must have told Nina the whole story because when he dropped Chloe at her house, she gave him a hug and said, "You'll find her. She probably needed to get away for a walk and lost track of time."

He thanked her and went home to start searching. His mom was on the phone again, and his dad, who was pacing back and forth, said she started calling around the neighborhood to see if anyone knew anything. He left them to it and started his own search of the paths on their property.

As soon as his mom finished making calls, he fully expected she and his dad would be out scouring the countryside too. He tried to keep his thoughts from going in one particular direction. He didn't want to come across his sister's body. He wanted to find her alive, but he knew what depression could do.

He took the easy paths first, the ones without many trees or vegetation. He took a quick walk around the farm. Then he went to the east and started up and down the paths his family made working and playing on the farm. Trees surrounded both sides of one path. He hoped she hadn't gone off the path in that part of the valley because it would be hard to see her if she went too far into the trees.

Close to noon, he started on the more complicated path, hurrying along the winding dirt road, more concerned than ever about Madison. He'd brought along water and took a few swigs from one of the bottles. The morning had been cool, but the sun was higher in the September sky, and it was getting warmer.

The trees along the route offered some shade. He looked first to his left and then to his right, trying to scan the ditches and look into the trees, so he wouldn't miss anything in his rush to find her. It would help if he knew what his sister was wearing. She probably had on her dark blue hoodie and jeans, but he couldn't depend on it. He walked slowly, and then he heard something that didn't blend into the usual country sounds.

He stood still for a minute, listening. The sound came again. A sniffle. He thought the noise came from his right but couldn't be sure. He started along the path again, looking more often to his right but also scanning the left.

Then he saw her a few feet ahead of him sitting against a tree. She must have heard his feet on the dusty path because she looked up as he approached.

Her forlorn look and red eyes tugged at his heart as she sniffled again. Her drawn face looked like it belonged to an old woman who had given up all hope.

"I couldn't do it," she said, holding up a steak knife.

He saw blood on her left wrist then, and his heart stopped for a second before starting to race. "Good." That was all he said before he walked over and sat beside her. He took the knife and set it farther away from her before pulling her into a hug.

She cuddled up to him. "It felt like the only thing to do."

"I suppose it did, but I'm glad you didn't do it. We all love you."

"I know," she said. "But I can't feel it. I can't feel anything. I don't have any energy, any belief that everything is going to work out. I don't have any friends at school. They all ignore me. I'm stuck at home with Chloe. I can't go out. But I don't want to go out. Who would I go anywhere with?" She started crying. "I thought I was done crying."

Jason wanted to point out that if Madison wanted to go somewhere, she could, but he knew what she meant. She felt stuck, and she couldn't see past this moment when the depression had such a hold on her.

"You need to get help."

They sat there silently for a time, then Jason pulled his phone out of his pocket and the other water bottle he brought along. "Here. Have some water. I need to call Mom and Dad and tell them you're okay."

She didn't object. She was listless, letting him take the lead.

Jason called his dad and told him he'd found Madison, and she was okay. He wouldn't go into the fact that Madison really wasn't okay. She wasn't in immediate danger now that he was with her. He told his dad they'd be back in about fifteen minutes and suggested his dad tell his mom to make eggs and bacon for Madison's breakfast to keep her busy.

Between her making breakfast and calling back all the people she'd talked to earlier, he figured they had plenty of time to get back to the house, but his dad might come out to meet them. He'd deliberately not told his parents where to find them, so as not to overwhelm Madison.

They couldn't go on this way any longer. She needed help. Maybe even inpatient treatment. They couldn't watch over her twenty-four-seven, and she needed that now. They would be headed to

the emergency room in Bismarck as soon as
Madison ate and showered.

CHAPTER 17

Samantha watched them walk back to the house. She spent a good part of the morning convincing Madison not to take her life. The teenager left the house around five that morning, and God sent Samantha.

Samantha knew of Jason's new relationship with Ashley. She'd noticed that God sent her to Earth to help anyone known to Paul's family who needed help. Usually that included pregnant women. Since Samantha had been at Chloe's birth, it seemed Madison also fell under Samantha's care.

Of course, Madison couldn't see her, but Samantha wrestled against the depression gripping Madison's mind.

Samantha had her own memories of depression from when she lived on Earth. She knew where the mind could go in the darkest moments. She'd felt worthless. Felt Amy deserved a better mother. Paul deserved a better wife. Her twin sister deserved a better twin. And on and on.

Her mind had gone in circles until she didn't feel much at all. She understood Madison. She was glad she could help in any way possible.

CHAPTER 18

Ashley got to class before Jason. She didn't realize how much she wanted to talk to him until she got there, and he wasn't there. When class started, and he hadn't appeared, she didn't know what to think. Had something bad happened with Madison? Jason had been so concerned on the phone the other day. And the way he had hurried out of class Wednesday to get home to be with Chloe showed how dependable he was with his responsibilities.

Her mind wasn't on the class. When it ended, she drove through a fast-food restaurant and took the food home to eat. She sent Jason a quick text to ask if everything was okay. He responded that he would fill her in when he had a chance. That reply worried her more.

When she arrived at work, the receptionist told her she and her supervisor were going to interview a patient who came to the emergency room.

As her supervisor, Dr. Beth Thorn knew Ashley wanted to work with younger patients. This seventeen-year-old would provide much-needed experience for her. Ashley hadn't told anyone from the school about her possible change in career. She'd only told Jason, Jill, and Paul.

They walked down the hallway talking about other things, not wanting to violate patient confidentiality. There wasn't much known about the girl at this point anyway. The father called and said they brought her in because of a suicide attempt, but that was the extent of their knowledge.

When they arrived in the emergency department, the receptionist admitted them to the locked patient area. A nurse came over to talk to them. Her name tag said Sarah.

"Hi, Dr. Thorn and Ashley. We can go into this area here, where no one can hear us talking, and I'll fill you in." She led them into a small office with a window looking out into the emergency room area.

She pulled up a chart on the computer on the desk. There were two chairs in the room, and Dr. Thorn and Ashley sat down.

"Madison is the girl's name. Her vitals are stable. She's in good physical condition and has a three-month-old baby."

"I understand she's seventeen," Dr. Thorn said. "Is the baby's father in the picture?"

"Doesn't appear to be. Her parents and an older brother brought her in. They look like a supportive family. They told me they've been taking turns staying with Madison, so she's never alone with the baby. Apparently, Madison has been to their local doctor, who diagnosed her with postpartum depression. The doctor recommended medication, but Madison refused."

At the mention of Madison, Ashley started to get a bad feeling. Was the patient Jason's sister? Her name was Madison. She had a baby, and she was seventeen.

Sarah continued, "One day, the brother found Madison on the front step crying, and the baby in the house crying. They started taking turns making sure someone always stayed with her. This morning she slipped out of the house before anyone was up and went out to the woods near their house. She took a knife with her to slit her wrist but couldn't go through with it. She's got a slight knife mark on her wrist, but that's as far as she got."

"Anything else we need to know?" Dr. Thorn asked.

"That's about the extent of it. I'll leave her in your capable hands. Dr. Wright said he will admit her if you think it's advisable."

"I'm already thinking that's going to be necessary. You can start searching for a bed for her and let Dr. Wright know we would like her admitted. I'll give you the go ahead when we're ready," Dr. Thorn said.

"She's in Room 5 now," Sarah told them.

She left them as they exited the small office, and Dr. Thorn headed in the direction of Room 5. Ashley followed behind and wondered what to do about the situation.

Dr. Thorn pulled the curtain back and held it for Ashley, who took one look into the room and stopped. Jason stood in the room with Madison. She was right. Madison was Jason's sister. She threw a smile in his direction, and then said, "Dr. Thorn, I need to see you out in the hallway for a minute. It's necessary."

Dr. Thorn looked at her strangely, and then followed her out of the room with a murmured excuse to the family. They moved far enough away from the room so they couldn't be heard.

"I know Madison's brother, Jason. I didn't realize at first when we talked to the nurse that he was her brother. Is that a conflict of interest?"

Dr. Thorn frowned. "How well do you know him?"

"We met in class last week. We went out for coffee after the first class and lunch after the second class. Other than that, a few phone conversations."

"You like him," Dr. Thorn said it as if it were fact, not a question.

Ashley's face heated. "Yes."

"Well, this is awkward." She stood there for a minute. "You can remain for the intake if the family approves. That's all you were going to do as an observer anyway. Someone else will be the counselor for her case. We'll ask them if you can stay in the room before we go any further."

"Okay."

They headed back into the exam room. Dr. Thorn took charge. "I'm sorry about the interruption. Ashley tells me she has known Jason for about a week from a class at school."

At this information, Madison lifted her head. Probably because the first part of this conversation wasn't about her. She looked at Jason.

He flushed as he became the focus of the group. "That's true. We met last week."

"There's a question of conflict of interest. I told Ashley if you were all okay with her staying for the intake, she could, and Madison will have someone else assigned to her for counseling. The intake will be the questions I'll ask right now, and the decisions we make for treatment now. After that, someone else will take over. Madison, it's up to you. We want to do what you want."

Madison smiled shyly at Ashley, and she smiled back. "It's up to you," Ashley told her. "Please do whatever you're comfortable with."

"You can stay." There was no hesitation in her voice.

"Okay." Dr. Thorn took over again. "We have six people in this small room. Again, Madison, who from your family would you like to remain here? If it's everyone, we'll have to move to a different location."

"How about my mom?" She looked at her dad and brother. "Mom can tell you everything. I'm fine with that, but Dr. Thorn is right. This is a little overwhelming to have so many people listening."

"Okay. We have a plan." Dr. Thorn stuck her head outside the curtain. "Do we have someone who can escort a few people to the waiting area?" she asked Sarah.

"Sure. I can do it." She stepped over to the curtained area. "Who's coming to the waiting area?"

"We are," Jason and his dad said in unison. They each gave Madison a hug.

"I'll call you as soon as I get a chance." Jason smiled at Ashley as he passed her on his way out of the room.

She nodded at him as he and his father followed the nurse to the waiting area.

Ashley appreciated the time it took to settle the room for the four of them. She had gotten over

her shock of finding out the patient was Jason's
sister and could concentrate on her job.

CHAPTER 19

Madison's mother had been looking at Ashley since she'd heard Jason and Ashley knew each other. It made Ashley nervous, but she pretended not to notice. Fortunately, as soon as Dr. Thorn started talking to Madison, her mother's attention returned to her daughter.

Ashley watched Dr. Thorn talk to Madison, who sat on the small gurney with the top of the bed raised. Dr. Thorn asked if she could sit at the foot of the bed, and Madison nodded. Ashley stood in the far corner to be out of the way as she observed.

Having gotten the preliminaries out of the way, Dr. Thorn asked, "Do you still feel like hurting yourself?"

Madison hung her head and whispered, "No."

"What are you feeling right now?"

Madison avoided eye contact. "I don't want to live, but I don't plan to do anything about it."

"Good." Dr. Thorn patted Madison's jean-covered leg. "What should we do in the meantime, so you can start feeling better?"

"I'd like to go home and continue on the way it's been." She peeked at Dr. Thorn through her bangs.

Her mom cleared her throat, and Dr. Thorn held up a hand to stop her from saying anything. "Is that working?"

"Well…"

"How old is your baby?"

"Almost three months old." She straightened a little on the bed, and a smile crossed her face.

"You love your baby, don't you?" Dr. Thorn asked.

"Yes. And I know some people hurt their babies when they have postpartum depression, but I would never do that. I would leave… I have left when I get too impatient with her."

"What's changed now? How are things going to be different? You've tried to change your feelings. Has that worked?" Dr. Thorn asked matter-of-factly. Her voice held no condemnation, just an inquiring neutral tone not likely to cause Madison to shut down.

Madison sat quietly for a few minutes. "I guess nothing has changed. I don't care what happens to me. I feel numb, and there's this darkness around me. Like the lights aren't on in this room. Does that make sense?"

"Perfect sense," Dr. Thorn assured her. "Normal for depression. But it's not normal to live every day feeling like that."

"Well, my mom got over her postpartum depression on her own. I thought if I waited long enough, mine would go away too."

Dr. Thorn turned her gaze in Madison's mom's direction. "You had postpartum depression too?"

"Yes. It lasted about a year. They didn't have as many treatments, and it wasn't understood or talked about much at that time." She looked at Madison. "You can trust Dr. Thorn. She seems sensitive to your feelings. If I had it to do over again, I would have tried treatment. I wish I had. I want that for you, but it's your choice."

Ashley appreciated how they treated Madison like the adult she nearly was. She was old enough to make her own decisions, but Ashley also wanted to shout, "You need to be an inpatient because you want to die, and you need to be on medication." She kept her mouth shut and waited to hear what Dr. Thorn would say next.

"What do you think of what your mother said?" Dr. Thorn asked.

"She's right. I didn't know it took her a year to get better. I don't want to wait that long."

Ashley heard Madison's mother let out a small breath.

"I believe we can find a medication that will help you. Would you be willing to try one?" Dr. Thorn asked.

"Yes, but I'm scared of side effects." Her vulnerability was obvious.

"What if you stay at the hospital a few days while we start you on a medication? The side effects usually show up early in treatment. The medication takes a longer time to help the depression. We can talk more once we know if you have side effects. We'll keep you informed what the side effects are, so you can decide what you want to do. You're making the right decision."

She stood up. "I'm going to go talk to the nurse about a room for you to stay in for a few days. Why don't you talk to your mom for a bit, and then I'll be back to see if you have any more questions?"

Madison nodded.

Ashley followed Dr. Thorn out of the exam room, and they went to the nurses' station. "You didn't give her a chance to say no to staying here."

"I know. I didn't want her to say no because we would have to commit her, and I didn't want to put her through that. At least she feels like she has some say in her treatment, but she's suicidal. She says she won't do anything, but she says she doesn't want to live. If something happened that stressed her more than she already is, who knows what decision she'd make. I don't want it to come to that."

Ashley watched Dr. Thorn talk to Dr. Wright about Madison's condition. As a psychologist, Dr. Thorn couldn't admit a patient to the hospital. Dr. Wright agreed Madison needed to be admitted and signed off on an order for admission to the Mental Health Unit.

Dr. Thorn finished her own charting of Madison's intake evaluation on the computer. They went back to Madison's curtained alcove and asked if there were any questions. The women both shook their heads.

"Okay. I'll get your medical plan together and come up to your room later to talk it over with you. Ashley will escort you to the room you'll be staying in as soon as the nurse comes by with your room number. We only let one person visit at a time. Your mother can go with you until you're settled."

Madison's mom stood up and patted her shoulder. "Thank you, Dr. Thorn."

"You're welcome." She left.

Ashley stood there as they turned in her direction. She smiled her reassurance, relieved when she heard the curtain being opened again. The nurse appeared and walked over to cut off the armband Madison already had on her wrist and put a new one on. She noticed Madison turned her hand downward, so they couldn't see the knife cut.

"I'll be going along with you," the nurse said. "My name is Sarah. If you didn't remember from before, that's okay. We'll stop by and pick up your brother and dad from the waiting room. They can go with us part of the way."

Madison smiled at that plan. She seemed close to her family.

Ashley pushed down a twinge of jealousy. She was getting together with Paul again, and soon Alex and Courtney. She should be thankful for her life, not envying a depressed girl who had a lot of courage.

They stopped at the waiting room, and Ashley motioned for the two men to join them. "Let's wait until we get into the hallway, and then we'll talk," Ashley said. Jason took a quick look at her before he focused on Madison.

They left the emergency room waiting area, and Sarah led them through the hallways. "Okay. We're going to the fourth floor. It's quiet in these hallways now with fewer people, so you can discuss what you want. Madison, do you want to say something?"

"I'm going to stay here for a few nights." She looked at Jason and then her dad. "The doctor said she'd start me on medication, and she'd tell me what to expect with side effects."

"Are you scared?" Jason asked.

"Yes, but I know this is the best thing to do." She looked down at her feet as they continued to walk down the hallway. "I scared myself this morning. I don't want to do that again."

Jason pulled her into an awkward hug because they were walking when he did it. "You'll be fine. We'll check on you often. You'll be home and feeling better before you know it." He let her go, and they continued on their way.

By the time Madison said a tearful goodbye to her dad and Jason and settled into her room with her mother, Ashley felt drained. Madison's mom could stay an hour, and then she'd have to leave. Ashley was glad she didn't have to be there for their parting.

They all thanked Sarah, who was ready to go back to the emergency room.

Ashley walked with Jason and his dad to the exit. She felt awkward and couldn't think of anything to say in front of Jason's dad. She was glad Jason had already mentioned calling her as soon as he could. She wanted to be a comfort to him.

"She's in good hands," Ashley told Jason and his dad at the hospital exit.

"You're right," Jason agreed. "Dr. Thorn seemed understanding."

"She is." Ashley nodded.

His dad shook her hand, and they both said goodbye.

Ashley returned to her office and found out that Dr. Thorn had already assigned a counselor for Madison and filled her in on the situation.

CHAPTER 20

Ashley arrived home to find the house empty and remembered Jill had the night shift. She took the time alone to regroup. When Jason didn't show up for class, she didn't know what to believe.

Then she was assigned her first patient to observe the process of admission, only to find out she happened to be Jason's sister. What were the odds? She felt bad for their whole family, but she liked how close they all seemed to each other.

Would Jason have more time or less now that Madison was an inpatient for a while? Dr. Thorn suggested Madison's stay would be a few days, but Ashley knew it would probably be closer to two weeks. It would take at least three weeks for the medication to have any effect, and since Madison planned to take her own life, they would keep her in the hospital if they could convince her to stay. She hated that the family might have to commit Madison if she decided to leave the hospital before she was ready.

The family appeared close, but committing a person to the psychiatric unit could create long-term animosity and conflict. She didn't want that for Madison or her family. She knew Jason figured high in the equation. She wondered how soon he would have a chance to call her. He probably had a lot of homework tonight and was taking turns with his parents watching Chloe. She would text him tomorrow if he didn't call her by the afternoon. It could be a simple *how are you?* text.

Ashley fixed herself a grilled cheese sandwich and considered calling Courtney. She wanted to stop by and visit her again when she had the time. Last weekend had turned out well, and she wanted to continue visiting before winter weather made the roads tougher to drive on due to ice or snow.

The pleasant September weather wouldn't last long. The changing colors on the leaves would make it a pretty drive to Chokecherry Valley, whether she saw Courtney or not.

Should she ask Paul to go with her? Or would Courtney feel they were plotting against her and Alex's directive? Ashley decided she'd go alone. When Alex was out of prison, they could drive down together. She texted Courtney she'd like to visit, and Courtney texted back to confirm it was okay.

The next day, the drive was as pretty as she expected. The leaves of some trees were green, but there were also many yellows, reds, and oranges. She felt a sense of peace wash through her as she thanked God for the beautiful day.

She started thinking about her brothers the closer she got to Chokecherry Valley. She didn't want to hold a grudge against them. She would find some passages on forgiveness in the Bible and study them. With God's help, she could get past these feelings of anger and hurt.

She should also send a text to Jason to ask how Madison was doing. She could check with him and see if he had time to get together and practice their speeches for class. She wanted an excuse to contact him and talk to him. Maybe she'd call him instead of text. She'd decide after she talked to Courtney.

She arrived at Courtney's house about one o'clock Saturday. When she knocked on the door, she didn't have long to wait for it to be opened.

Courtney smiled at her in welcome. "Come in."

Looked like Courtney had gotten the message that Ashley wasn't going to be put off any longer. They were family, and they were going to spend time together like a real family. Fights and all. She smiled.

Courtney settled on the couch. "Have a seat. Do you want anything to drink?"

"No, I'm fine. I drank a soda on the way here. I do appreciate that you are letting me visit."

Courtney laughed, and her face lit up. "Like I had a chance against you once you made up your mind. Did anyone ever tell you you're tenacious?"

"A time or two. I did respect your request to leave you alone for two years. I was younger then, and I didn't know any better. Hopefully I've learned a lesson about how little time we all have."

"You're being philosophical today."

"Can't help it," Ashley said. "I've been taking a class about sibling relationships, and here I am. Trying to be supportive."

Courtney settled back against the couch and grabbed a throw pillow, which she held on her lap. "I know, Ashley. Probably more than you realize. I have five siblings. I can't imagine not seeing one of them for two years. You held out longer than I expected. Alex and I weren't fair to you. I regret that."

An apology? Ashley certainly hadn't expected one. She'd always gotten along with her sister-in-law and been crushed when she was ignored. They'd said it was for her own good. She didn't agree.

"We didn't want to taint you with Alex's mistakes. You were off at college, and we felt you'd be better off concentrating on your dream job and forgetting about us."

"Forget? Yes, I'm going to forget my brother I've grown up with and lived with, who I was close to, and who I confided in because Mom and Dad dumped us wherever they could. Yes. I was going to forget him. And you. I considered us friends, and while I know Alex was the driving force in the decision to cut me off, you went along with it." She took a deep breath then stood and paced. "I guess I needed to get that off my chest."

Courtney smiled in a gentle way, not sneering. "We deserve that and more. We were young too, and it was the wrong decision we made. We assumed you'd have Paul."

Ashley laughed bitterly. "Yes. That turned out well too." Then she plopped down on the recliner. "Paul and I are patching up our relationship."

"Seems like this class you're taking is bringing out your feelings and resolving some things."

"Well, I am studying psychology. I suppose I should get my own life together."

They sat in silence for a while.

"I'm glad you're back, Ashley. I missed you." Her expression showed a mixture of regret and sympathy.

"I missed you too. I wanted to be there for you and Alex." Ashley knew she sounded whiny.

"We know. Alex withdrew in prison. He didn't want to see anyone he knew except me. He felt my own family would support me, and they did. I missed you though. You were a big part of our life, and then you were gone. You don't know how much I wanted to open the door when you started pounding on it back then."

"I thought you found it easy to ignore me." Ashley heard the bitterness in her own voice.

Courtney frowned. "No, it wasn't easy. I almost went against Alex, but then I knew he'd ask me, and I didn't want to lie to him. He'd already been lied to by too many people."

"What do you mean?"

"Nothing important." Courtney shrugged it off. "It was tough for him being a bank manager. I don't know what he's going to do when he gets out of prison. He'll definitely be making a career change. Obviously, no bank is going to hire him."

"No, probably not." Ashley hesitated, and then jumped in, "If you two need financial help, let me know."

Courtney started to interrupt.

"No, let me finish, and then I'll bring it up once to Alex. After that, I won't bug you about it. I have enough to share. If this has left you short of money, I'll help. The offer is always there, but I won't bring it up again. You don't have to squirm."

Courtney stilled at her words. "We're fine, but we appreciate it. I'm speaking for Alex too. I know he'd agree."

"Okay. New subject. Do you have to work today?" Ashley asked.

"No, I'm off. Next weekend I do have to work. You might not want to make the drive."

They laughed together.

"I'll call before coming, unless you stop seeing me. Then I'll be the persistent knocker on your front door again," Ashley said.

"Not necessary. We're past that."

Ashley stood up. "I think so too. Well, I won't keep you any longer. Next time we'll talk about books or something lighter. Enough of the serious subjects."

"Sounds good." Courtney followed her to the door. "Thank you, Ashley."

Ashley waved from the front step. "Sure."

She looked down the street at the grocery store and the other small businesses. Maybe she'd stop and get a few items from the store, and then she could go straight home from here. She moved her car the short distance to the front of the grocery store, parking behind a pickup. It was an old blue farm pickup and brought back memories of riding in the bed of one during her younger years.

She got out of her car, and as she got to the door of the grocery store, it opened. Jason stood there. She stepped back to let him outside.

"Wow. Another surprise sighting," Ashley said.

"Do you want to talk for a minute or are you in a hurry to do your shopping and get back to Bismarck?" he asked, holding the door open.

"I can talk." She smiled at him. "I have plenty of time."

He smiled back and let the door close behind him. He went over to the old pickup with his groceries. After putting the bags onto the passenger seat, he closed the door. "Were you visiting Courtney?"

"Yes. We've come to an understanding, and I think we'll be close again. It looks like the class I'm taking is helping me move forward." She pointed to the house at the end of Main Street.

"Oh, right. Of course." He nodded. "I'm glad it's working out for you. I like Courtney and Alex. I always got along with him too. No judgment here." He stared straight at her.

"Thanks for saying that. I appreciate it." Ashley wasn't sure what to say next. She had so many questions and not a lot of time. He must need to get back home. "How did Madison do overnight?"

"Okay, I guess. We only get to see her for two hours in the evening because there are activities during the day. Of course, that's during the weekdays. The activities, I mean. And you probably already know this because that's your area at the hospital." He put his hands in the pockets of his jeans. "That was crazy running into you at the hospital yesterday. I never expected it."

"You don't need to worry I'm going to share any information about Madison with anyone. You and I can't even talk about what happened in the emergency room unless Madison signs a release or brings it up. They assigned another therapist to treat her anyway. Maybe you already met her. I'll be happy to listen to your side of things. Of course, it's all up to you," Ashley assured him.

"She hasn't been in the hospital long enough for anything to change. I guess we'll wait and see. Mom did get an update from the doctor this morning over the phone, and it looks like Madison did okay overnight. She starts the medication today, and we're hoping the first one works. I looked up information online, and it said sometimes they have to try a few different pills before they find the right one, and then they have to try different doses." His lips drooped, and he suddenly looked tired. "It's a long process, isn't it?"

"Yes. I'm sorry, Jason. I wish Madison had decided to get help earlier. She didn't, and so we go from here. She's in a good place."

He straightened his shoulders. "Yes, she is. What did I miss in class on Friday, besides you?"

"Well, you got to see me anyway." She smiled at him. "Just more information on the different types of speeches. Nothing that isn't in the books. There's a signup sheet for when you want to give your first speech. Three different people give speeches per day with discussion after each speech." Her lips twisted. "I really don't want to give one. I wish there was some way out of this class." She sighed.

"Do you still want to get together to practice your speech?" Jason asked.

She felt another smile cross her lips. "I'd like that. Do you have time?"

"I'll make the time. How about tomorrow? I'm going to be in Bismarck to visit Madison, and we can get together after that. Would that work?"

"Definitely. I don't have anything except homework the rest of today. If we meet tomorrow, it will force me to write the speech. I want to give it in class as soon as possible and get it over with," she said.

"Sounds good." He moved away from the passenger door. "I'll text you and check if the time works for you once I know when I'm visiting Madison."

"Sounds good." She took a step toward the store.

"We go to church every Sunday morning, so I know it won't be until after lunch. I must admit, I don't read the Bible otherwise. I do pray and beg God for things to change."

Ashley smiled. "Me too. I should start thanking Him for more things He's given me and include them along with all the asking."

He laughed. "Good idea. I'll adopt your philosophy too."

"Well, I should let you get going. You probably have things you need to get into the fridge, and I should get my groceries and start back to Bismarck."

"Yes. I'm on babysitting duty when I get home." He went around to the driver's side of the vehicle and looked over the top of the cab. "I'll text or call to check about meeting tomorrow when I know the time."

"Sounds good." Ashley went into the grocery store and looked around for the few things

she needed. It felt good to talk to Jason, even for a short visit. Her heart sang. She'd see him tomorrow. It almost made writing the speech palatable.
Almost.

CHAPTER 21

Saturday afternoon, Ashley worked on writing her speech. She often found herself daydreaming about Jason and how he'd looked in Chokecherry Valley that morning. Finally finishing the speech, she picked up her tablet to read her library book.

When Jill returned home from work, Ashley was happy to be distracted by conversation with her.

Ashley prepared a salad for both of them, and they sat at the table eating. "Do you want to tell me what's bothering you?"

"Your decision, or lack of a career decision, has got me thinking about my own future," Jill said. "I'm not sure I want to work on the Labor and Delivery floor any longer. You know I can't have children, and that's making it harder to be happy for other mothers every day. And on the days when a mother loses her child, I come close to falling apart."

Ashley reached across the table and gave her friend's hand a comforting squeeze. "I always wondered how you did it."

"I wasn't going to let my feelings win. I love babies, but now it's too much. Other options are available for nursing jobs, and my plan is to transfer to another department. Telemetry and the Kidney Dialysis Unit both have openings. I'm leaning toward Telemetry. I'm pretty good with broken hearts." She smiled at her own weak joke.

Ashley smiled back at her. "Especially mine. Look what you did for me. Made me face my fears with my brother and nudged me into a relationship with Jason."

"Oh, please!"

Ashley was relieved to see Jill's eyes light up.

"I knew you were crazy about that guy from the moment you first mentioned him. Even over the phone, your voice got all trembly when you mentioned Jason."

Ashley flushed. "Glad you found that amusing."

"I didn't. I found it sweet and nice. I worry about you, you know. That's what best friends are for."

"I worry about you too. I'm glad you told me what's been bothering you. Try out Telemetry. If you don't like it, there's always another department. You know the hospital is so short of nurses, you have your choice of departments."

"You're right," Jill agreed. "Now, I'm going to have a relaxing evening with my book."

They took care of the dishes and settled in the living room, each reading her own book.

#

Sunday morning, Ashley's mind kept wandering to Jason and the tired look on his face outside the Chokecherry Valley grocery store. She wished she could do something, but only time would help the situation. At least Madison was getting the help she needed.

Jason showed up about 3:00 p.m. to practice their speeches. Jill was working again, so they had the place to themselves. Ashley was happy to have the privacy. She didn't want to practice in front of two people at once. As she told Jason, she'd already had trouble just speaking in front of Jill last night when she went through her speech with her.

They settled across from each other in the living room. Ashley sat in the chair across from the couch where Jason sprawled in his usual slumped position. Maybe he was uncomfortable with his height. Or he was tired from everything that had happened, and that was how he sat when he was relaxed.

She wished she felt as relaxed as he looked. "Do you want to go first?"

"Sure." He sat up and took the backpack off the couch where he'd dropped it when he sat down. He searched inside and brought out a notebook. "I wrote it out instead of putting it on my tablet. I'll enter it into the computer and print out a nice copy when I have the final version worked out."

"I do that too. I like to cross things out on paper and make little notes, and then rewrite it again." She settled back against the stuffed chair. Since he was going first, she could take a normal breath.

"Okay. Let's stay sitting for the first time through. Here goes." He read the speech without looking at her once. When he finished, he folded the paper in half.

"That was good," Ashley said. "In fact, it only needs a few minor tweaks, and you'll be ready."

He finally looked up. "What do I need to change?"

She found the slight flush on his cheeks cute but kept that opinion to herself. Her face was going to be fiery red when she finished her own speech. He probably wouldn't think her cute at that point. "You've got it down pretty well."

She picked up a pen from the coffee table that was positioned between them and reached out her hand. "Give me your speech, and I'll show you the two places you hesitated."

He handed it to her.

She leaned forward, set the paper on the coffee table and made a few marks on the paper. "Look here."

He leaned forward, so their heads were close together. She found the closeness distracting but told herself to focus.

"You see this spot here?" She pointed to a pen mark by one of the sentences. "If you take out this word, it flows better. Same thing at this other place." She had crossed out another word.

He read both sentences out loud with the changes she'd suggested. "You're right. It sounds better." He read the whole speech from his seat on the couch, looking up a time or two to get her reaction.

She smiled at him. When he finished, she said, "Perfect."

"Now you," he said.

She took a deep breath and let it out slowly as she picked up her paper from the coffee table. She'd been working on the speech all morning since she got home from church and believed it sounded okay when she read it.

She followed Jason's example of sitting down through the first reading. He made one comment of a change when she was finished. She made the change and read it through again.

"Perfect," he said.

She laughed. "Okay. I guess we have our reading down. Now we need to actually stand up and do this. Along with some eye contact and inflection."

He smiled at her. "I guess so."

It helped her that he had some doubts about his speech too, which wasn't really fair. She should be hoping that he was calm. The saying "Misery loves company" came to mind.

They practiced for another hour, and then both had enough. She'd turned red a time or two, but she could remember most of the speech without her paper by the time they were finished. The instructor was allowing them to use their paper or tablet as a crutch for the first speech. After that, they had to memorize all the other ones.

"We're ready for next week," Jason said as he stood at her front door to leave. "If you want to practice before next week, we can do it over the phone. There are plenty of times when I'm watching Chloe, and she's asleep, so I can do other things."

"That sounds good. Same here," Ashley said. "You can also practice more with me if you want to do that."

They said goodbye, and Ashley stood by the door for a minute after he left. The apartment suddenly felt lonely without him there.

#

Jason managed to have lunch with Ashley the next few times after their class met. They enjoyed getting together, but they hadn't found an evening when they were both free for a date. They each gave their speeches and did a passable job. Both flushed red and stumbled, but overall, Jason said he was happy with his own performance. Ashley just wanted to get through the class, and as long as she passed, she didn't care how high a grade she received.

She got out of bed early on Monday, excited to see Jason at class. She hoped he would have time to have lunch with her, but she kept her expectations low.

When she arrived at the classroom, he was already sitting at his desk. He smiled brightly at her. "Hi."

"Hi. How's it going?" she asked as she settled at the desk beside his.

"Great. We had a good weekend."

Dr. Williams walked into the room, and she didn't feel she should talk about anything personal in front of him or the other students.

135

After class, she took a longer time than she needed to get her stuff together. She hoped Jason would ask her to join him for lunch.

Instead, he walked her out of the classroom and stopped on the sidewalk by the entrance to the building. "I'm sorry I can't get together today. It's my turn to watch Chloe."

"I'm sorry too." She certainly felt let down, and his eyes were shadowed with fatigue as they stood there for a minute.

"My parents had something they had to do today, so I have to get home," Jason said.

"That's understandable, Jason. You've all had a rough time. I know you'll make it through this. I pray for you and your family," she said, feeling shy at telling him.

He grinned down at her. "Thank you. That's the best news I've heard besides Madison coming home soon. I better get going. I'll see you on Wednesday."

"Bye." She watched him walk down a different sidewalk from the way she went. Obviously, Madison's condition still concerned him, so it was good that she was still in the hospital. Ashley walked along the path to her car. The bright sky and beautiful September colors lifted her mood. She considered what work might bring today. The people they saw in the clinic interested her, but could she deal with people's problems day after day?

She supposed, given the fact her parents had been largely absent, even when they were in the same house, she would find a career helping other people appealing. Especially since she'd been lonely.

Her upbringing kept her from trusting others and from getting close to them. She was always afraid they would leave her. Paul hadn't helped when he'd told her to get out of his life. Alex basically did the same thing when he went to prison. She hoped to quickly change his mind when he returned home.

Courtney was someone she hoped she could reconnect with now the ice was broken over the prison thing. Jill had been in her life since Ashley had started living at her grandmother's house. It was nice having one close friend who understood her.

She should try to set up more times to see both Courtney and Paul. She'd have time to make and hopefully keep friends now that she was nearly done with school. She'd call Paul first to meet up with him again.

She finished work for the day, went home and called Paul. They planned to meet the next evening. He asked if he could bring Hannah. Since Ashley didn't have anything personal to talk about with Paul, she agreed. She wanted to meet Hannah anyway.

#

Tuesday arrived, and Ashley did housework in the morning before she went to work. She got an hour of homework done for her class on

Wednesday. Work passed quickly, and before she knew it, it was time to meet Paul and Hannah.

She wasn't as nervous as she had been when she saw Paul again for the first time. As long as his mood stayed stable this evening, which it should since he wasn't drinking, she was okay. He would be on his best behavior for her to meet Hannah.

They agreed to go to the same bistro where they met previously. It might become their spot.

She'd dressed in black jeans, black ankle boots, and a long-sleeved light blue sweater. Once the sun disappeared from the sky, it would be chilly outside. The sky darkened as she headed out of her apartment.

She was the first to arrive, and the waiter led her to a table. She faced the entrance, so she could see her brother and his girlfriend arrive. The waiter was setting out three menus and filling her water glass when Paul came in with Hannah.

Hannah was average height with shoulder-length blond hair. Her bright smile showed a happy young woman, the kind of woman Paul needed in his life. A moment of jealousy struck Ashley before she pushed it away. Maybe someday she'd meet someone who made her that happy. She ignored the memory of Jason's face as it popped into her head.

"Ashley, this is Hannah. Hannah, Ashley." Paul waited until they shook hands and then helped Hannah remove her lightweight coat. She wore a pink sweater that gave her face a glow in the dimly lit restaurant.

"I'm excited to meet you, Ashley. Paul has talked a lot about you and the adventures you and Alex had when you were growing up," Hannah said.

"Well, he wasn't as happy about them when we were younger." Ashley grinned. "I admit I instigated most of our escapades. Poor Alex. He didn't want me to leave him behind, even when I started getting into girly stuff like makeup. He refused to try the makeup—except one time. We did have a picture of him wearing blush and mascara and one of mom's dresses, but he might have gotten rid of it by now.

"Most of the time when we stayed in Chokecherry Valley, I liked to climb trees. When I stayed at my grandmother's house here in Bismarck, I was quieter. I read a lot." She didn't add that she didn't want to upset her grandmother and get sent back to Chokecherry Valley. She wanted to stay in high school in Bismarck, so she behaved herself. She realized now she'd stifled her real inclinations by doing that. She'd built a habit of pushing away her more adventurous side.

"Hey there." Paul touched her hand.

"Sorry." Ashley smiled at them. "I was having a few memories."

"That's okay," Hannah said. "I paint pictures for fun, and, sometimes, I'll miss whole boatloads of information Paul shares. I'm busy imagining how the landscape would look better with a certain lighting."

"Oh, that's wonderful you paint pictures. I always thought it looked fun. I'm not creative. I tried to draw for a while, but the drawings didn't look like anything when I finished them."

"Oh, I don't do very well. My proportions can get all out of whack. Like I said, it's fun."

Paul reached over and squeezed Hannah's hand. "It doesn't matter as long as you like doing it."

"Have you painted a picture of Paul?" Ashley asked Hannah.

Hannah laughed. "I tried once when he napped on the couch. I drew a picture first because I didn't want to wake him up by dragging out all my painting supplies. He wouldn't let me do it if he knew, so I kind of snuck into the room and drew him with pencil and paper. It looked like a man, but not much like Paul."

"It was wonderful. I keep it on my fridge," Paul said.

"Like a child's drawing," Hannah said wryly but didn't look upset. "Paul told me you're almost finished with your bachelor's degree in psychology."

"Yes. I have two classes this semester along with a two-week long clinic observation class. I'm excited to be nearly finished. I'm tired of studying every night, but at least I don't have much homework in the classes I'm taking now."

"What classes are you taking?" Hannah asked.

Ashley decided to avoid mentioning the class that focused on siblings. "I'm taking Oral Communications. It's a freshman-level class I should have taken a long time ago, but I put it off."

"You always hated to speak up in a group," Paul said.

"Yes. That hasn't changed at all. I'm still scared to get up in front of the class. Oh, here comes the waiter. Do you know what you want?" Ashley asked, relieved to change the subject.

"What's good?" Hannah asked.

"Pretty much anything on the menu. I don't think you'll be disappointed."

After they ordered, there was a lull in the conversation. Ashley didn't find it awkward at all. Hannah seemed like a nice woman, and she was happy for Paul. There appeared to be a real closeness and contentment between the two, something she never noticed in Paul's marriage with Samantha.

With Samantha, there had always been sly digs against Paul. Little barbs and arrows flew through the air. Their discontent had been exacerbated by both of them drinking.

The conversation flowed with general information on each of their jobs, and once the waiter delivered their food, they all dug in with gusto.

"You're right," Hannah said after a few minutes of silence while they all ate. "This is excellent. I'm coming here more often."

Ashley was relieved Hannah liked the restaurant choice. She was always nervous when she chose the place to eat. "I'm glad."

Paul put down his fork. "I was going to wait until after we finished eating, but I can't wait any longer."

Ashley had taken another bite. She was afraid the food would get stuck in her throat when her mouth suddenly went dry. What did Paul want to say?

He glanced at Hannah. "What do you think?"

She put down her fork too. "Sure. Go ahead." She smiled at Ashley.

Ashley breathed a sigh of relief when she realized where this was going. Paul had mentioned that he already bought Hannah a ring. Hannah must have finally decided it was time to accept his proposal. She smiled back at Hannah and then looked at Paul. "What's up?"

"Hannah has agreed to marry me."

"Congratulations to both of you. I couldn't be happier." She picked up her water glass and gestured to the two of them. "I guess we're going to toast with our water?"

They did. There were laughs and more smiles all around, and they picked up their forks again.

"I didn't see a ring on your finger, Hannah," Ashley said.

Hannah's grin got bigger. "Oh, you looked," she teased Ashley.

"Of course. My brother wants me to meet his girlfriend and can't even wait a week?" Ashley laughed at Paul's sheepish expression. "I looked."

Hannah dug in her purse and unzipped a side pocket. She pulled out the diamond ring with a silver band and handed it to Ashley.

Ashley looked at the beautiful square cut with smaller diamonds around it. "It's gorgeous."

"Thank you." Hannah put it on her finger. She looked momentarily shy, like she wasn't used to showing it off.

"Have you worn it to work yet?" Ashley asked.

"No. Paul and I agreed to show you first, and then I'd wear it."

Ashley felt the hint of tears in her eyes. "That's sweet." Her face was starting to hurt from all the smiling she'd done that evening. "When we're finished and standing up, you're both getting big hugs from me."

When the meal was over, she didn't forget.

CHAPTER 22

The next few weeks sped by for Jason. He spent time watching Chloe, taking his classes online and in person, doing homework, and visiting Madison at the hospital when it was his turn. He was amazed they'd managed to keep her in the hospital for two weeks.

She wanted to come home the day after they admitted her, but gradually her pleas to come home diminished. They all somehow convinced her to stay until she started feeling better. God must have had something to do with it because it was a miracle she stayed. The doctor hoped for one more week before they released her.

On the last day of September, Jason realized he could ask Ashley to have lunch with him after class. He didn't have to get home immediately for a change. They talked before and after class, but he was always in a hurry to get home to help.

They hadn't even had time to practice their second speeches. He knew she was signed up the same day he was, because they had coordinated it in class. They were scheduled for next week.

He felt bad about always rushing away after class, but he'd told her he was busy. She knew about Madison and Chloe. He didn't know if she understood the time those commitments took. Did she think he wasn't interested in her any longer?

There was only one way to find out. He dressed casually but more neatly than usual before he headed for class. He parked in the parking lot he knew Ashley used. It would give him more time to talk her into lunch if he needed to persuade her.

When Ashley walked into the classroom, Jason made sure to send her a bright smile. He babbled away nervously. Ashley gave him a curious look, and then class started.

He felt foolish. No doubt she thought he had lost it. He hadn't given her a chance to say anything or respond in any way.

Class seemed to drag on for longer than fifty minutes. When it was finally over, he grabbed his stuff and stood by Ashley's desk while she stuck her notebook into a folder and put on her jacket. He forced himself to concentrate. "Are you busy today?"

She eyed him closely. "Don't you have to get home and take care of Chloe or something?"

"Not today. I finally have a break. I assume you have to get to work, but I wondered if you have time for a quick lunch before you have to leave." He spoke quickly, trying to get the words out before she left.

She looked at him for a minute and smiled. "It sounds like you want to go to lunch today. I have time. In fact, I have all afternoon. I finished the clinical observation at St. Gertrude's. I just have to put together a paper for the class. Let's go to the place we went to before. They had fast service."

He let her go before him as they left the classroom. He couldn't hide the big smile on his face as he followed her. His pulse slowed down to a more normal rate. She'd agreed, and she'd smiled. She didn't seem mad at him for how long it had taken him to meet with her.

They stepped outside, and she rummaged in her purse for her sunglasses. "How is Madison doing?"

"Great. We were lucky. The first antidepressant looks like it's working. We're hoping she'll agree to stay at the hospital one more week, and then she'll be home again. It feels like she's been gone forever."

"That's great, Jason. I'm glad for her and for you too."

"She sounded more like her old self when I visited a few days ago. I didn't realize how much I missed her being happy."

"Life has been rather chaotic for you lately, hasn't it?" Ashley asked sympathetically as they reached the parking lot. Jason shrugged and nodded. "Pretty much a mess. I'll meet you at the restaurant, so we can both leave from there."

"See you in a few minutes." Jason waited until she'd backed out of her spot and followed behind her in his own vehicle to the restaurant.

Once they were seated and ordered, Ashley asked, "Will Madison be able to settle in once she gets home?"

"I'm concerned about her regressing, but I'm taking it one day at a time. Something I've learned to do more lately than ever before," he said.

The waitress set down their order and asked if they needed anything else. Ashley shook her head. When they assured her they had everything, she left. Ashley started eating immediately.

Jason scooped up his own burger and took a bite. He should try harder to see Ashley in the evening sometime when they could have a real date. Sure, he'd been concentrating on family things, but come on. He could find the time.

"Is something wrong?" Ashley stared at him in concern as she finished her salad.

He picked up his burger again. "Sorry. I zoned out there for a minute." He took another bite of his burger to give himself time. She wouldn't expect him to talk with his mouth full.

"I said life might return to a more normal pace for you once Madison is discharged from the hospital. You won't be running to Bismarck in the evenings to visit her," Ashley said.

He swallowed and answered, "Maybe there would be another reason to come to Bismarck in the evenings. Maybe if you're free some evening, we could go to a movie or something."

She pushed her plate over to the side and leaned forward. Her eyes sparkled. "Are you asking me for a date?"

"Yes. I want to date you. I'm getting old, Ashley. I'm not into playing games. I could pretend I don't like you or play hard to get, or whatever people do these days. However, I'm a straightforward guy. Life has been complicated with a lot of things since we met, so it took me a while to get my act together. Now that I've realized I want to spend more time with you, I don't want to waste time. So, yes, I'm asking you out."

"Okay. The answer is yes. I'd like to go out with you too. I find your honesty refreshing." She looked down at the table as he picked up his burger again.

"I have something else to ask you." She looked up at him again. "I have been left and abandoned a lot in my life. I'm nearing thirty also, and I'm not into games either. I'm finally getting my relationships with one of my brothers and my sister-in-law back on track. I can't handle a relationship with someone who runs hot and cold."

"Like I have." His food sat heavy in his stomach. "I believed you understood how busy I was with Madison, Chloe, homework, and farmwork."

"I understand, but sometimes I need the words. You can call. You can text. You can send me an old-fashioned letter. Somehow, you need to communicate why you're busy. I don't want to wonder when you're going to get back around to me since you have all those other commitments. Am I making sense?" She leaned back and crossed her arms over her chest.

"Yes. I promise to be more forthcoming from now on," Jason said.

"That's all I ask." She smiled at him. "On the topic of dating, let me know when you have a free evening, and we'll plan our date. Either call me, or we'll have lunch again after class and discuss details." She patted his free hand where it lay on the table.

"Let's plan now," he said.

They agreed on a date for the following Tuesday. They were going out to eat.

CHAPTER 23

The doctor discharged Madison from the hospital over the weekend, and everyone used the time to adjust to her return home. She spent most of her time holding Chloe. The family continued to keep an eye on her.

Jason tried hard to trust Madison enough to leave her alone, but he couldn't let go yet. Neither could his parents. He noticed there was always someone around, and they scheduled it so Madison wasn't left alone. It looked like it would take time.

They tiptoed around the situation and tried not to make it obvious to Madison. She would probably notice at some point. For now, she seemed blissfully unaware as she took care of Chloe and enjoyed being home.

They talked briefly about whether she would return to school in a week, but she hadn't decided. She also had the choice to study at home for the G.E.D. high school certificate.

Jason hoped that would be the route she took. In one way, he saw how it would be easier for her, but she'd have no reason to leave the house on a regular basis, which was the one downside to studying online. She needed to make friends somehow.

She continued twice-a-week therapy with the counselor she'd had at the hospital. Once they were sure Madison was stable, they would transfer her care to a local therapist. Maybe then he could relax his vigilance.

#

Ashley looked around her and Jill's apartment Saturday. The place needed a thorough cleaning. She'd focused on studying and getting through the week and wasn't used to having an entire Saturday free.

As a psychology major, she found it ironic she was so unsure of herself with interpersonal relationships. She didn't have a lot of self-confidence in her appeal but should follow the advice she gave to others: practice liking yourself.

Jason seemed comfortable with himself. Well, most of the time. She had made him nervous before he declared he wanted to date her. She found that endearing. It was nice to know she wasn't the only shy one when it came to dating. Plus, speaking probably wasn't going to be his favorite thing to do either.

Ashley industriously cleaned the apartment during the morning but decided the afternoon was too beautiful outside to not enjoy it. She got out her camera and headed on her favorite scenic drive. She found a stream about five miles out of town she liked to take pictures of in different seasons.

Most of the leaves had fallen from the trees since mid-October arrived. In a few months, the ground might be covered with snow. The stream

150

usually froze by mid-December because it was shallow.

She parked off to the side of the road, keeping her flashers on to alert other motorists. Since she'd been coming here for about four years, she'd never seen another vehicle drive by.

Ashley found it strange her parents never associated with the other families in Chokecherry Valley. Her mother inherited the house on Main Street from her parents but only visited Chokecherry Valley on occasion. Her parents had lived in Bismarck since Ashley's mom went to high school.

Ashley didn't have any idea why her father agreed to sell their Bismarck home and settle in Chokecherry Valley, making it their home base. Maybe they decided, since they were traveling most of the time, there was no need to make friends in Chokecherry Valley.

She realized now how their decision cut her off from being close with the other people in Chokecherry Valley. She'd visited Alex and Courtney occasionally, but since Alex went to prison after three years of being married, she hadn't been there until her recent visits with Courtney.

Alex would have a hard time coming back to the house in Chokecherry Valley when he got out of prison. As the previous bank manager, he must have known a lot of people in town, and they'd all know what he'd done. Courtney's job definitely brought her into contact with most of the residents of Chokecherry Valley. What could Alex do for a job? No one was going to hire an ex-con in a small town.

She took her pictures and started driving back to Bismarck. She wanted to go see Jason, but she knew now wasn't the time. Madison needed to settle into a routine with her family.

She waited until she got home and then texted Jason. "How are you?"

She tried not to keep looking at her phone, wondering if she missed the chime of an answering text. In the meantime, she pulled out the book she'd checked out from the library days ago. She'd try to read again.

About fifteen minutes later, she got a response. "Doing well. Madison's settled. She's playing with Chloe," Jason texted. "I'm nervous about her."

"That's normal. Soon you'll be more relaxed about the whole situation," Ashley responded. "What are you doing?"

"Did chores, now I'm watching them have fun while I try to study. I'm working on my next speech. I hope you want to get together again and practice."

Ashley felt warmth slide through her veins. "I'd like that. You got me through the first one. Since we have to memorize the next one, I'll need even more practice."

"Me too. We'll have to get together a lot." He laughed. "Can you tell I want to spend time with you?"

He didn't wait for her to answer. "I do want to spend a lot of time with you."

"That's good. Me too." She found it easier to say it over text than in person.

"Okay. It's a plan. I need to get back to my homework."

"I have to finish my paper, so I can be done with that clinical observation class. Can't wait to see you."

"Same here," he texted. "See you Monday."

"See you then."

She put away her phone and picked up her book. She finally got into it about a half hour later when she stopped thinking about Jason every other minute.

CHAPTER 24

Ashley dressed in black pants and a black sweater with a three-strand golden chain necklace for her date with Jason. Her calmness surprised her. They'd been in class together now for almost two months. Besides that time and their meetings for lunch, this wasn't the first time she'd be alone with him. It would be the first time they'd be alone at her place without the distraction of homework. He might want a kiss. She didn't know if she was ready for that intimacy yet. She'd decide how she felt if the time came. She pushed it out of her mind.

Jason arrived on time, and she didn't make him wait. Opening the door, she took a deep breath at the sight of him. He wore his usual jeans and had chosen a button-down, open-necked shirt instead of his usual t-shirt. His hair looked recently combed, and whatever cologne he used smelled citrusy.

She felt more in this moment than she'd felt for him the whole time they'd been sitting beside each other in class. She knew everything had now changed between them. He was going to be in her thoughts constantly, as if he weren't already a big part of them.

"Hi," he said, smiling at her and shifting from foot to foot. "It's great to see you all dressed up. Not that you don't always look good. You do, but— I'm expressing myself very badly. You look nice."

"It's fine, Jason. Thank you." She smiled back at him, noting his nervousness. "You look quite handsome." She was floored by her feelings for him. She finally got her act together and invited him into the apartment, glad she'd done a thorough cleaning over the weekend.

He pulled his hand from behind his back and held out a beautiful bouquet of yellow and orange mums and other fall flowers in a gorgeous crystal vase. "These are for you."

She noticed his hand trembled as he waited for her to take it from him. Her smile widened. "Thank you. They're gorgeous. Choose a seat if you want or wander around. I'll put these on the coffee table here, so we can all enjoy them."

"All?" he asked, looking around the room. He didn't sit down either.

She suddenly felt short beside him. "My roommate, Jill, would be the other one enjoying them. She's visiting her mother this evening. She'll be home by nine at the latest. Her mother is getting older and doesn't stay up much past ten."

"I see."

Ashley wondered if Jason took that as a warning she wouldn't be alone tonight if he wanted more than a kiss in the hallway. He didn't seem like that kind of man, but they hadn't had any intimate moments since they met. Practicing speeches didn't count. She'd been more nervous about them than spending time with Jason. Until now. They'd always been in a hurry to get to their next commitment.

"Are you ready to go?" he asked.

"Sure." She grabbed her black beaded purse from the couch. The mild late October evening didn't require a coat yet. "Where are we going?"

"I found this wonderful Italian place. Do you want to go there? If you prefer somewhere else, that's fine with me," he said.

"No. Italian sounds good."

He led the way to her front door and opened it for her. She stepped through and then waited for him to step out into the hallway, so she could lock the door. Once they reached his car, he opened the front passenger door and closed the door once she leaned back against the seat.

While she strapped on her seatbelt, she got an even better feeling for Jason. He certainly had manners. It didn't look put on for her benefit either. He probably held doors for his sister and mother too.

When he pulled out of the parking spot, he said, "The restaurant is about ten minutes away."

She laughed. "Most things are only ten to twenty minutes away. Except the colleges. Both are a little farther, depending on traffic. It's nice to live in the middle of town."

"I like the size of Bismarck," he said. "Have you come up with a plan yet after you graduate in December? Is it more school or a job?"

"I've given it a lot of reflection. I still haven't made up my mind and have another month before I need to sign up for next semester's classes. If I continue. At least I've already been accepted for the program, so it's my choice. If I decide I'm done with school, I'll job hunt. If the right job comes up here in town, I'll stay. If not, then I'd consider moving. I don't know what I'd do for a job. I guess I'd look at the openings and see what interests me.

"It's just not like me not to have a plan. I'm a planner by nature. A lot depends on what happens with my family situation."

"Meaning?" he asked.

"I'm starting to get to know Paul again after a separation, and Alex…I guess I don't have to tell you what happened with Alex, since you live in Chokecherry Valley."

"When we're seated at the restaurant, I'd like to hear all about it, Ashley. Gossip isn't always accurate, and I hope you're okay with telling me what's going on with your family."
He laughed. "You already know half of what's going on in my family, since you've met Madison and my parents."

"Yes. I can't believe that happened in the emergency room. I don't know anything about your parents though."

He parked in the restaurant's lot.

"And," she smiled at him when he looked over at her to see what she wanted to say, "you haven't shown me any pictures of Baby Chloe. As a proud uncle, I know you have at least one."

He grinned back at her. "We'll be hunched over my phone and ignoring the food all night if you want to see pictures of her."

He got out and opened the door for her again, even though she could have been out of the car before he walked over to her. She knew it would please him to be helpful, so she waited. It made her feel taken care of, which she enjoyed. No one had waited on her since her grandmother, and only on special occasions when Ashley was a teenager.

When they were seated at their dimly lit table, Ashley looked around. "I like it."

The room felt small but appeared to have plenty of seating. The candles on the tables and the lower lighting made it seem cozy. Her mouth started watering at the wonderful smells of garlic and oregano wafting around the room.

"What's good?" she asked Jason.

"I'm a fan of their lasagna. Do you have a specific Italian food you usually eat? It's all good here." He set his menu to the side. "Don't hurry on my account. I already know what I want."

He sat there quietly while she perused the menu. He seemed relaxed. She realized she liked that quality about him the best. She knew that was an exterior view. He had not been so calm about Madison, and Ashley had seen him agitated on a few other occasions. Even then, he appeared dependable.

She should wait to start cataloging his good qualities until after she decided what to order. She'd never been this distracted by a man before. When she was a teenager, she'd swooned over boys, but she had been too busy pursuing a career lately.

The waiter arrived with their waters. When he asked what they'd like to drink, Jason ordered a soda. He asked her if she wanted wine with her meal. She shook her head and ordered coffee. They both ordered the lasagna, and the waiter left.

Ashley said, "Let's see a few of those pictures before the food comes."

He pulled out his phone, and with a few swipes, brought up a cute picture of Chloe smiling up at him with big brown eyes and held it out for her to see.

"Oh, she's so cute. She has your beautiful eyes." Ashley felt her face flush, and she suddenly felt shy.

Jason smiled gently. "Thank you."

He handed her his phone. "Keep scrolling. Most of the pictures are family."

She looked through them, occasionally stopping to ask him to identify the people she didn't know. He had pictures of his mother, father, Madison, and Chloe. She recognized Paul's in-laws, Nina and Frank, and remembered they were Jason's neighbors. Ashley looked closely at all the pictures. She had a feeling she'd be seeing Jason's parents at their house soon.

She handed his phone back as the waiter brought their food. "You have a lovely family."

"Thank you."

They settled their plates and took a few bites. It was hot and delicious. "I want to keep eating," Ashley said, "but it's too hot. I need it to cool off for a minute. I've already burnt the roof of my mouth." She put some food on her fork and held it away from the rest of the plate to let it cool, so she could eat. She didn't want to stop. "I can't believe I've never eaten here before tonight."

"You've been busy. I'm happy I got to bring you here first." He grinned at her.

"Me too." She went back to eating little bites until her food cooled enough to take another bite.

They talked about work and school during the rest of their meal. Once they finished and refused dessert, they settled back to get to know each other.

"How were your meetings with Paul?" Jason asked.

"We've gotten together a few times lately. I met his fiancée, Hannah. She's nice. I'm looking forward to having her in the family."

Jason looked surprised. "Have they made it formal then?"

"Yes. I guess they just got engaged. It's news to most people."

He twisted his water glass back and forth. "She came out and visited him a few times at Frank and Nina's house during the summer. She seemed pleasant, but I didn't talk to her much more than to say hello in passing."

"We should probably keep it to ourselves until Paul has a chance to tell Alex and Courtney," Ashley said.

"I heard Alex will be coming home soon. When is that?"

Ashley didn't sense any distaste in Jason's voice. She'd wondered if he would bring up her younger brother. "He's being released December first. Paul and I will give him and Courtney a few days to settle in, and then we'll visit. I'm worried about his reception in town. Do you know how people are going to treat him?"

He paused before answering, and she was relieved he took the time to consider it through.

"For the most part, it's water under the bridge. In the end, what he did didn't affect a lot of people. The only problem is there are people who believe his boss, Steve Hanson, might not have had a cancer relapse if he hadn't had to deal with the disgrace of being the one who hired Alex."

"What do you think? Obviously, I want to know if there will be any awkwardness between you and Alex."

Jason's response could be a deal breaker.

"I'm totally okay with it. He's gone to prison and paid the price. I don't know the details, and it's not my place to judge."

"What about what they're saying about Steve Hanson?"

He pushed his water glass away. "I happen to know Steve had cancer before the embezzlement happened. His course of treatment worked, and he recovered from the cancer. Alex isn't to blame for the relapse. Cancer is unpredictable."

"That's good. It would about kill Alex to think what he did caused someone else that kind of pain."

"You were close with Alex?" he asked.

"Yes. Up until he went to jail. Then he and Courtney, in their infinite wisdom, refused all visits from me and Paul." She couldn't hide the bitterness she continued to feel over their actions.

"I'm sorry. That must have hurt." Jason's voice was soft and comforting.

"It did. It was another rejection. It's recently I found out they did it to save me from the anticipated fallout from Alex's actions. I wish they'd let me make up my own mind. I was certainly old enough to decide for myself. Besides, I don't live in Chokecherry Valley, so it wouldn't have been difficult for me."

Jason sat there quietly for a minute. "You may be underestimating people's reaction at the time to what Alex did. Yes, it's been two years since it happened. At the time, there were nasty things being said about him. If you heard them, you would have felt the need to correct their impression, and that wouldn't have done anyone any good. You might have said things you regretted in the heat of the moment, and you can never take back what's said."

"Well, I wanted to defend him," Ashley said stubbornly.

He smiled. "You seemed like such a softy, but you have a tough center. Alex knew. He did what he believed best."

"Well, I have something to say to you. I expect, if we continue our friendship, you'll allow me to make my own decisions." She clenched her fist on the table.

Jason's expression turned serious. "Definitely. You're a grown woman. Your choices are your own."

Her fist unclenched. She smiled at him. "You're a smart man."

"And about Alex. I've always liked him. I'll continue to be pleasant and courteous to him when I see him. Unless he turned into a bad guy while he was in prison."

She laughed. "I'm sure he hasn't changed."

The rest of their conversation was less serious, and they finally left the restaurant. The drive back to Ashley's apartment passed silently.

With a flutter of nervousness in her stomach, she wondered if he would kiss her goodnight. She snuck a peek at him. His mouth was set in a firm line of concentration as he pulled the car up to her apartment entrance.

"Do you want to come in for a while? I'm sure Jill won't care. She's probably home by now."

He turned toward her where she sat in the passenger seat. "I do want to meet Jill sometime, but it's been a long day. Do you mind if I take a rain check?"

She felt her heart sink. He wanted to leave. "Sure. Some other time."

He reached out with his hand and touched her cheek. "I'd like to kiss you."

She took a deep breath, surprised at his openness. She was ready for that kiss.

"But," he continued, "It's too soon."

"Too soon?" she protested. "We've known each other for two months. That's acceptable for one small kiss."

He smiled at her.

She could get sidetracked by his smile easily, but she wanted a kiss.

He leaned forward, leaving his hand against her cheek. He placed a kiss on her forehead.

She pushed his hand away from her face but laughed. "Okay. Fine. On date two, we are going to kiss."

"How do you know there will be another date?"

"Because you like me, and you respect me. And I like you." She reached up and patted his cheek with her hand, then removed it from his face and opened the car door before he could react. "Let me know when you're free for our second date." She laughed again and slipped out of the car.

She knew he watched until she got into the apartment building. She waved from the doorway before she closed the door and headed upstairs to update Jill on her first official date with Jason.

CHAPTER 25

Paul picked up Ashley the following Saturday morning. He'd changed his mind about waiting until Alex returned home before he visited Courtney. Ashley called Courtney and told her they were coming to visit, and Courtney didn't object. Paul wanted to visit Frank and Nina while they were there, so they agreed to lunch at their house.

Ashley wanted to fit in a quick stop at Jason's house to see his family again. She hoped having Paul with her would ease the atmosphere. She'd texted Jason they were going to be in Chokecherry to visit family and might stop by his house.

He sent back a quick text with a thumbs-up emoji.

Ashley smiled. He might think it wasn't a big deal, but she had no idea how his mother would feel. Would she want to clean the house, or was she laidback and took things as they came? Probably the latter. With Madison's ups and downs, she'd probably learned to let go of unimportant things, such as a spotless house.

It was nice to have company on the drive to Chokecherry. She'd brought along her camera to take a few pictures. Since it was November now, the trees had lost all their leaves. They hadn't had much snow yet, so the landscape had a stark brown look. The temperature was in the forties, wonderful for this time of year.

She and Paul talked about Hannah, Ashley's work, and a bit about Jason.

"He seems like a nice guy," Paul said. "I'm glad things are working out."

"It's early days yet," Ashley said. "We've only been out on one official date. We see each other in class three times a week and go to lunch afterwards."

She remembered the text she got from Jason yesterday. He'd set up another date for the coming week, and she looked forward to it. And the kiss he promised. This time it wouldn't be on the forehead either.

Paul laughed. "Sounds like more than one date to me. All those lunches." He glanced at her.

"That's what I thought too." She smiled back at him. "He's cautious. I'm cautious. There's no hurry either."

"No, there's not. Better to take time and be sure." Paul concentrated on the road. They turned off the highway and onto the gravel roads.

She wondered if he thought about Samantha, but she didn't say anything. It wasn't any of her business. Paul's first wife put them through a lot, but Paul hadn't been blameless. Now she was gone, and Paul had Hannah.

"Are you okay if I set up a lunch with Hannah sometime? I'd like to get to know her."

"No, I don't have a problem with that. In fact, it's a great idea."

"Good. We'll have a great time talking about you without you there."

"I'm sure you'll come up with plenty of stories from our youth." He pulled into Courtney's driveway.

Courtney sat on the rocker on the porch. She waved as they got out of the car.

"Isn't it chilly to be sitting out here today?" Ashley asked. Sure, forty was a good temperature for this time of year, but not warm enough to sit outside on the porch without a fire pit going.

"I came out about a minute ago. The house was too warm from the oven being on this morning. Hi, Paul." She stood up to go into the house with them.

"Hi. It's great to see you again." He didn't hesitate but went up to her on the porch and gave her a firm hug. "It's been too long, but I'll forgive you."

Courtney glanced over at Ashley. "You two are definitely from the same family. It's great to see you too, Paul. And you, Ashley."

They followed her into the house, and Ashley took a deep breath of the lovely scent wafting from the counter. "You made blueberry muffins."

"Yes. I'm in a baking mood, and since I had a warning you were going to make frequent visits now, I figured it would be a good thing to feed you once in a while." She sent Ashley a sly glance.

"Yes. I get it. I stormed the castle before, and I don't regret it a bit."

Courtney smiled. "I don't either. I'm going to blame these visits on you and Paul. Alex can blame you for breaking the guidelines we set up."

"Fair enough," Ashley said. "I'm happy to take the heat."

They ate muffins and laughed together. They left right before lunch and went to visit Paul's in-laws.

Nina and Frank had a surprise for them. They arrived to find Jason, Madison, and Chloe there also. Ashley was happy his parents hadn't come too. It was enough to see Jason and his sister and niece.

Before Ashley knew it, Madison hugged her, and then she found herself holding Chloe.

"Looking good," Paul whispered in her ear.

She would have jabbed her elbow into her brother's side if she had her hands free. She settled for a subtle glare. Then she was distracted by Chloe. The baby felt so soft and comfortable in her arms, and she had an epiphany. This was what she wanted to do. Take care of children. In a group and one at a time—preschoolers of all ages.

While she sat there holding Chloe, she started having visions of starting a daycare. She'd find a business place to rent and use some of the money her parents had given her to start the daycare. She knew she'd have to update any place she rented. She'd have to get certifications for the building and for herself and maybe take some more classes to run the daycare.

"Hey there," Jason said.

She jumped at the sound of his voice. "Hi."

"You were sure deep in thought," he said.

She glanced around and found that conversation around her continued, but she and Jason were getting a few looks from the others. She realized they believed they were being subtle. She smiled up at Jason. "Yes. I made up my mind about something. I'll tell you later."

He appeared ready to question her, but then he said, "Okay. Do you want to join the others in the kitchen or stay here?"

"I'd rather stay here with Chloe. She's so cute. I'll go see if the others in the kitchen want any help."

"You can take Chloe with you." Jason smiled at her. "Then all the women will be in the kitchen."

"That better be a joke because any man in my life better expect to be helping out in the kitchen," she warned.

"Oh, you don't need to worry about that. My mother has already trained me to make meals and clean up after myself," Jason said.

"That's good." Ashley got to her feet, still holding the baby. "I'm going to the kitchen now, only because I choose to." She flipped her curly hair back with the hand that wasn't holding Chloe.

"Don't worry. I'm sure Nina will have the men clean up after we eat. Plus, we'd all offer anyway. That's the way it is."

Ashley left to join those in the kitchen, leaving Jason in the living room. Nina was directing Madison on setting the table while she scooped mashed potatoes into a bowl and set out a plate of pork chops. A salad and several dressings followed. Once the food and place settings were ready, the men were called from the other room.

Ashley gave them credit. They asked if they could help with the meal, but Nina told them they were fine. They could help clean up after the meal, she told them. They hadn't protested. All of them were used to Nina's way, just as Jason had assured Ashley.

The lively lunch featured a lot of laughing and talking. Ashley sat by Jason, and Chloe lay in her car seat, happily playing with a hanging toy.

After they'd eaten, the men stayed in the kitchen and cleaned up after the meal. Ashley found herself sitting on the couch in the living room. There was a gorgeous corner fireplace. It wasn't lit now, but she could smell the recent smoke from it.

After Ashley talked to Nina for a while, Madison came into the room with Chloe. She walked over to Ashley. "Would you like to feed her?"

Ashley hadn't noticed the bottle in Madison's other hand. "Sure." She reached out for the baby.

Once Chloe settled in her arms, Madison handed her the bottle. "I changed her diaper, so she should be fine for a while."

Chloe latched on to the bottle, and Ashley stared at her in wonder. Her brown eyes were wide open and stayed focused on Ashley's gaze. "She's a beautiful baby."

Madison flushed. "I love her so much." She glanced at Nina. "Do you mind if I say something to Ashley?"

"No, that's fine." Nina started to get up, but Madison stopped her.

"You can stay. It's nothing private."

Nina nodded and settled back into her rocker.

Madison sat by Ashley on the couch and played with Chloe's little socked feet, avoiding eye contact. "I wanted to thank you for what you did the day I came into the emergency room. You were so kind to me. I was scared, and you were calm."

Ashley smiled at Madison and would have given her a hug if she hadn't had Chloe in her arms. "You're welcome. You deserve to be happy. I hope things are better for you now."

Madison looked up, her expression serious, and finally made eye contact. "Yes. I feel a lot more like myself. I even smile occasionally."

"Good. You'll be okay. You have a wonderful family, and it looks like Nina and Frank are good friends."

Madison looked at Nina. "They are wonderful. All the times they've taken care of Chloe have been so helpful. I know Mom is grateful too. We couldn't have done it without you and Frank helping."

Nina smiled back at her. "We love you and that little one. Any time you want us to watch her, we will."

Ashley looked down at the baby in her arms. "You're a special little person with all these people loving you."

"She's added another admirer," Jason said from the doorway.

She knew he'd arrived in the room because she'd felt a shift in the atmosphere. Oh, she was so in trouble with her feelings for Jason.

"Of course I'm an admirer. Who wouldn't be?" she cooed at the baby. She had fallen in love with Chloe the minute she held her. A feeling of warmth ran through her, and she realized that when she started her daycare, she'd be able to continue holding little babies, and playing with and teaching little children. It was the perfect answer to the question she'd been asking herself since the summer. Did she want to stay in psychology? The answer was no. She wanted to work with children but in a different capacity.

The other men came into the room behind Jason, and Paul said, "I t's about time to get back, Ashley. You'll have to say goodbye to your new love."

Ashley bent over the baby and softly said goodbye. She had a sneaking suspicion Paul meant Jason, but she ignored him. She'd give him a hard time on the drive back to Bismarck.

Madison reached over and expertly took Chloe from Ashley's arms then looked around the room. "I'm glad I got to see you today," she said shyly.

Everyone returned the sentiment.

Ashley hadn't had another moment alone with Jason since right before they'd eaten, but maybe that was best. They parted with the comment they'd see each other Monday in class. She knew they'd have lunch afterward. She was disappointed they hadn't talked much today, but she was looking forward to their next date and, hopefully, a kiss.

#

Soon Paul and Ashley were in the vehicle to go back to Bismarck. Paul drove.

"Can we stop at Courtney's again for ten minutes?" Ashley asked him as they left the farm's driveway.

He looked at her in surprise before looking back at the road. "Sure. Did you forget something?"

"No. I just want to ask her something. Since we're here, I may as well do it in person."

She knew he thought it a weird request, but he didn't comment any further other than to agree. She hoped Courtney was at home. If not, she would have to ask her the question on the phone.

They pulled into the driveway behind Courtney's vehicle. Ashley tensed up and reconsidered. Maybe she didn't want to ask Courtney in person.

"Looks like she's here," Paul said.

"Good." Ashley opened her door. "I'll be right back."

She hurried up to the front door, and Courtney opened it as Ashley reached out to knock.

"I didn't expect to see you again today." Courtney stepped aside to let her in. "Isn't Paul coming in?"

"No. I have a quick question and hoped I could ask you. Do you have a few minutes?"

"Sure."

They both stepped into the house, and Courtney closed the door. "Do you want to sit down?"

"No." Ashley twisted her hands together as they stood inside the front door. "I'll make this quick. How did you know you were in love with Alex?"

Courtney's mouth dropped open, and she stared at Ashley. Then a grin quickly came and went. "That's an interesting question. I won't leave you waiting for an answer. When things progress a little further in your relationship with Jason, I'll give you a hard time about this conversation." A grin appeared again. "I knew something was going on when I saw you talking to him outside the grocery store the other day."

"Courtney, I don't have time." She knew her face was flushed. She was glad it was winter, and when she stepped outside, Paul would attribute her red face to the cold air.

"I knew I was in love with Alex almost right away. We had a lot in common. I was attracted to him, and I felt in my heart he was a nice guy. We just clicked. Most things we did together were easy. Not that we have a perfect relationship. No one does. I wanted to impress him, but I didn't have to. Does that make sense?"

"Yes. Thank you." She turned back to the door, wanting to leave now that she had her answer.

Courtney didn't stop her. She opened the door for Ashley and said, "If you ever want to talk, feel free to call. I was lucky enough to have sisters, but a sister-in-law like you is the next best thing."

Tears came to Ashley's eyes, but she held them back. She reached out and hugged Courtney, who hugged her back. "Thanks," she choked out and hurried out the door.

When she got in the vehicle, she was grateful for the warmth. Paul had left the pickup running while she was talking to Courtney.

"Are you okay?" he asked as he backed out of the driveway and started driving down Main Street to exit town.

"I'm fine. Courtney gave me a hug before I left, and it made me emotional." She wasn't about to tell him what they talked about in the house.

"Okay." He drew out the second syllable, like he knew there was more, but he didn't press her.

She was grateful for his restraint. She had so much to pray about. Jason, for one. Her new realization that she was either falling in love with him or in love with him already. It was all so new to her. She had been so excited when she first saw him at Nina and Frank's house, but then really disappointed when she didn't get to spend any time alone with him. She wasn't sure of anything, except she wanted to spend all her time with him. She hoped he felt the same way she did.

Second on her mind was her new career in child care. She just knew that was what she wanted to do when she graduated. Holding Chloe had been eye-opening to her. The experience had suddenly made her realize how much she loved children. She didn't know where she'd start a daycare, but she finally had a direction. She had a lot of thinking to do.

She realized Paul had been quiet while she was doing all of this thinking. She looked over at him and caught his swift gaze.

"Still okay?" he asked with a wrinkle in his forehead and a concerned look in his eyes.

She smiled at him. "You can relax. I'm fine. It's nice of you to care."

"I do." He smiled back at her.

"I know. It's sweet." She leaned back in her seat and relaxed. "I was planning my career choices. I've decided I don't want to be a psychologist, but I do want to work with children."

"Hey, that's great. What career do you want with children?"

"I'm going to start a daycare, but I have a lot of research to do. How to be a certified daycare center, or whatever the proper term is. What I need to do with building code for rental places, and all that stuff. I'm excited." Her smile got bigger. It was such a relief to have a direction again.

"I can see that. You're practically bouncing on the seat, now that you're back in the present. I thought I'd have to yell in your ear when we got you home, so you'd come back to earth," Paul said.

"Not necessary. So, when do you want to get together again?" she asked.

"I'll have to look at my schedule when I get home. Hannah has me signed up for a few things."

"Glad she's keeping you busy," Ashley said, content to see the happy smile on Paul's face.

"Me too."

"If you're interested, how about coming over with Hannah on Thanksgiving Day? Or does she have family?" Ashley almost regretted asking. What did she know about cooking for a holiday?

"She's got a sister. I'll check with her about Thanksgiving and let you know."

CHAPTER 26

November passed quickly, and Jason and Ashley continued to get together after class for lunch and to practice their speeches. They were unable to find an evening or time for a second date. Finally, they decided to get together in the evening on Thanksgiving Day at Ashley's apartment. Jill was going to be out of town for the holiday.

Jason would spend the day with his family. Nina and Frank's daughter, Abigail, and son-in-law, Mark, were visiting Paul's in-laws. Courtney would be celebrating the day with her family. Paul and Hannah had agreed to come to Ashley's apartment for a dinner meal at 1:00 p.m.

Thanksgiving arrived quickly, and Ashley tried to get everything done in her small kitchen. Hannah agreed to bring a salad and dessert. Ashley had never cooked a turkey, and she began to perspire in the hot kitchen. She opened the window above the sink and started doubting she could pull off this meal. What had she been thinking?

She should have agreed with Paul and let him and Hannah host the meal. A knock on the door interrupted her anxious musings, and she looked at the clock on the stove. Who could that be on Thanksgiving Day? It was too early for Paul and Hannah.

She opened the door to find Hannah standing on the other side with a big smile on her face. "May I come in?"

Ashley's heart sank, although she couldn't help but smile back at Hannah. "Certainly."

She stepped back and let Hannah in. "You can set those on the island," she said to Hannah when she realized Hannah was carrying her meal offerings.

Hannah set a pumpkin pie on the island and put a bowl of pasta salad in the fridge, along with whipped cream. "I know I'm early, so don't panic. Paul and I discussed it, and we decided I might be able to help you. We knew if we called, you'd say you had it all handled."

Ashley stood there for a minute; her feelings all jumbled. She'd been so stressed this morning and now realized she had family who cared. She burst into tears.

Hannah came over, put her arms around her and hugged her hard. "It's okay. I know it's been tough for you for a long time, but you're not alone any longer."

Ashley leaned against her, and it took a while to stop crying. Eventually, as the soft wool of Hannah's coat finally penetrated her consciousness, she realized she hadn't even taken Hannah's coat. She pulled away. "I have to get some tissues. Why don't you take your coat off? It's stifling in here. You must be roasting faster than my turkey." She laughed. "I'll go change and wipe my nose."

She headed toward her bedroom but turned around in the hallway before she reached her door.

Hannah was unbuttoning her coat. "Thank you. I guess I needed that."

Hannah grinned at her. "We could all use a good cry now and then. I've done it plenty of times, believe me. Now, go do whatever you need to get ready. I'll be fine watching things here in the kitchen. When you get back, we'll settle down with a donut and something to drink."

"You brought donuts? Oh, Hannah. I love you. No wonder my brother proposed."

Hannah laughed. "Go."

After Ashley's rocky start to the day, she had fun with Hannah. Before Paul arrived, she and Hannah got to know more about each other. Ashley was pleased with Paul's choice. They had a lot in common.

Hannah cut off parts of the turkey and put them in a separate pan, so at least some of the turkey would cook in time. She helped peel potatoes and set the table.

Ashley had bought a beautiful autumn floral centerpiece. It all looked lovely once it was ready. There was a lot of eating and laughter during the day.

When they left, Ashley gave Paul a hug, which he returned wholeheartedly. "You made a wonderful choice," she told him. "Hannah's what you need."

"Thanks. I agree," Paul said.

Ashley turned to Hannah. "And thank you. For everything." They also hugged goodbye. When they left, Paul's arm was around Hannah's shoulders.

Ashley looked around her apartment. They had helped clean up before they left. The apartment was ready for Jason's arrival. Hannah left the pie and whipped cream for her and Jason to have an evening snack. Ashley smiled. Hannah was so kind.

Ashley had an hour before Jason would arrive. She went into her bedroom and studied the clothes she wore. Would they work for an evening with Jason? This was their second official date. She studied the clothes in her closet, looking for something that made her feel good when she wore it.

She found an amber sweater and a pair of worn blue jeans. She debated on shoes. She finally decided to wear a pair of blue socks and forget shoes. She felt comfortable and stylish at the same time. She knew Jason probably wouldn't even notice. She combed her hair until it shone. She was ready.

She wandered around the apartment for the next half hour, unable to settle. He arrived about fifteen minutes late, but she didn't hold it against him. Judging holiday traffic was difficult, and Chokecherry Valley was about an hour away.

When he knocked, she took a deep breath and let it out. This was it. She felt it was a momentous occasion. She opened the door.

He smiled and held out a gorgeous red poinsettia in a pot. "Hello."

"Hi. Thank you. These are beautiful flowers." She set the pot on the island.

"It's for an early start to the Christmas season," Jason said.

"Let me take your coat." She was so happy to see him. She remembered what Courtney told her about falling in love.

He pulled off his black puffer coat, which she threw on a chair in the living room. At least she got that part right, and she didn't feel like crying since she'd gotten it out of her system with Hannah's help.

"Let's have a seat in the living room," she suggested.

He sat on the couch.

She chose a chair across from him, even though she wanted to snuggle up next to him. "How was your Thanksgiving?"

"Busy. Why is it that the same people who get together every day can be busier on Thanksgiving than a normal day?"

"Because you spend time together. Otherwise, you're all doing your own thing."

"True," Jason said.

"What did your family do today?" Ashley asked.

"We played games before we ate. Then my dad and I watched football until he fell asleep in his chair. Then I watched alone. Madison and Mom took a walk while I watched Chloe," Jason said.

"Madison seems to be doing well."

"Yes. I'm definitely happy with the way she's feeling. Is it weird that I keep waiting for something to go wrong?" he asked.

"No. It's normal. You had three months of chaos before she got help. It takes a while to get over that," Ashley assured him.

"You're right. What did you do today with Paul and Hannah?"

"We ate and talked and laughed. It's the first time I spent much time with Hannah—or Paul, in a long time. We had fun." She considered the day, pleased with the happiness she'd seen on their faces. "I'll ask Hannah out for lunch in the new year."

"That's great. I'm glad you two are connecting," Jason said.

"Yes. I'm really happy with Paul's choice. On a different subject, I realized Alex is returning home next week. His release date is December first," she said.

"How do you feel about that?"

"I'm so excited. It's going to be hard to wait until he's home a little while before I go and see him and Courtney."

"Things worked out for you and Paul. I'm sure it's going to be okay with Alex and Courtney."

"You're right." She decided that was enough talk about her brothers for today. "Do you want to do something tonight?" she asked.

"Sure," he agreed.

"What did you have in mind?"

"How about a movie here at your house?" Jason asked. "And you can come join me on the couch and snuggle while we watch."

She could feel his eyes practically drilling into her brain to see what she thought. "I'd love to do both."

Ashley grabbed the remote from the coffee table and plopped down right beside him. "I've been waiting for you to ask me to come over here."

She was elated he'd suggested snuggling. She planned to make sure she got a kiss before he left. She wanted to ask him how he felt about her, but at the moment, she couldn't come up with a subtle way to do that. Maybe she'd be blunt if she didn't come up with subtle.

Without hesitating, he put his arm around her. She leaned into him.

"Before we start the movie, I'd like to tell you what I was thinking about when I was holding Chloe at Frank and Nina's house the other day." She didn't believe he was going to have any problem with her career change, but she felt the need to tell him right away. Mainly because she wanted to share her excitement.

"Is everything okay?" he asked with concern, his brow wrinkled in concentration.

She considered it as his "thinking face." "I want to start a daycare. I love little children and decided that would be the perfect place to start a career."

He hugged her closer. "That sounds perfect for you, Ashley. I'm so happy that you're happy with your choice."

"I am," she said, reveling in the feel of his arm tight around her.

"Great! I also have something to say to you, Ashley," he said with a tremor in his voice. He was focusing on her face and almost looked afraid. "I really like you a lot. I haven't had a lot of girlfriends in the past. Mostly because I never found someone who interested me enough to date for very long. I feel different about you. I like you a lot, and I'd really like it if we spent more time together. I'd like it if we would date exclusively. What do you think?"

She felt his hand shaking when he picked hers up and held it. She knew her own hand was trembling too, and her heart beat faster than she felt was healthy. "Yes. You're the only man I want to date." She looked up at him, willing him to kiss her now.

He leaned forward and kissed her on the lips. It seemed to go on forever until she felt dizzy. Then it ended too quickly. "Hey, why'd you stop?"

"I needed to breathe." He laughed. His expression relaxed.

She did notice he was breathless. Well, she was too. "The kiss was worth waiting for, but let's do it more often."

"Definitely."

They watched a movie, but she wasn't really paying attention and couldn't have described it when it was over. There had been a few more kisses during the movie, which hadn't helped her concentration.

When he was ready to leave, she got another kiss at the door. "See you tomorrow," he said as he held her in his arms.

"We don't have class tomorrow because of the holiday." She looked up at him with a smile and raised brows.

"I know." He smiled down at her. "But I need my Monday-Wednesday-Friday lunch with you. Any objections?"

"No. I could spend time with you every day. What about you?" She waited breathlessly for his answer.

His smile grew bigger than she'd ever seen, and when he gazed at her, the light in his brown eyes stole the rest of her heart. "I'd love to spend every day with you. We'll plan that out tomorrow when we see each other." He stole another quick kiss and left.

She leaned against the closed door. Her heart felt full. A Thanksgiving to remember forever.

~ ~ ~

Read the final Chokecherry Valley book in the
Richmond Sibling series.

<https://www.jeanrezab.com>

Chokecherry Valley Faith
Richmond Siblings Series –
Picture of Book 4

**Grace and goodness light the way in this
inspirational, contemporary story of forgiveness
and family.**

Alex Richmond is being released from prison after a two-year term for embezzlement. His former boss's cancer has returned, and the town blames Alex.

His wife, Courtney, looks forward to his return.

But how will the community react?

Can Alex and Courtney work as a team after having been apart for two years and face the trials that will come with his return home?

The conclusion of the Chokecherry Valley Richmond Siblings Series will bring the biggest surprise of all.

COPYRIGHT

ABOUT THE AUTHOR

Jean Rezab writes from her home in North Dakota. Having grown up on a farm, she enjoys all things country, especially wildflowers, wheat fields, and winding lanes.

An excerpt of her writing has appeared in Humanities of ND Magazine. She likes to entertain her readers with mysteries and women's fiction containing messages of love and forgiveness.

Her favorite authors while growing up were Mary Higgins Clark, Agatha Christie, and Debbie Macomber.

www.ingramcontent.com/pod-product-compliance
Lightning Source LLC
Chambersburg PA
CBHW021439150726

47989CB00001B/307